MYS
F
DEW

Dewhurst

Dear Mr. Right.

Dear Mr. Right

By Eileen Dewhurst

Dear Mr. Right

EILEEN DEWHURST

A CRIME CLUB BOOK

DOUBLEDAY

New York   London   Toronto   Sydney   Auckland

A CRIME CLUB BOOK

PUBLISHED BY DOUBLEDAY

a division of Bantam Doubleday Dell Publishing Group, Inc.
666 Fifth Avenue, New York, New York 10103

DOUBLEDAY and the portrayal of a man
with a gun are trademarks of Doubleday,
a division of Bantam Doubleday Dell
Publishing Group, Inc.

Library of Congress Cataloging-in-Publication Data

Dewhurst, Eileen.
    Dear Mr. Right / Eileen Dewhurst. – 1st ed.
        p.   cm.
    "A Crime Club book."
    I. Title.   II. Title: Dear Mister Right.
PR6054.E95D4   1990
823'.914–dc20   90-32474
                                                       CIP

ISBN 0-385-41442-0

For Joan Vickers, gratefully

CHAPTER ONE

"And this, Fiona, is James!"

The arched tips of his hostess's red talons slid down James's sleeve and dug into his wrist, guiding his hand upwards.

"James! How lovely!" Fiona's fingers moved against his, telling him right away that this was one of the ones out for his body rather than his mind. He still hadn't decided which type was the more tedious. "How come we've never met?"

"Perhaps you don't buy books."

"Buy books?" Perplexity stilled the busy fingers.

"James owns and runs Better Books," interpreted his hostess, arresting her departure on the realization that she was leaving them alone together a little prematurely. "At least you must have *seen* it, Fiona darling, it's got the best facade in Linton."

"Of course I've seen it." The fingers were back at work. "I'm not quite the mindless creature you take me for, darling."

"I don't think you're mindless, darling. Just lucky enough to be too busy to read. Fiona models, James!"

"How interesting." James hoped the response didn't sound as flat as it felt. The thought that he was due a minimum of three hours in Fiona's company made him all at once overwhelmingly tired. But this was how he always felt sooner or later at these impossible dinner parties for which invitations so regularly came— sitting at his desk or moving about behind his long, clear shop windows, known to be widowed and well off, he was an inevitable social target for those ladies of Linton to whom it was a matter of self-respect to have the latest piece of highbrow fiction prominent in their sitting rooms. He couldn't refuse them all and retain the sympathetic image he was well aware helped his business.

"It can be interesting." Fiona smiled meaningfully.

"I'm sure." He had forgotten what they were talking about.

"Better Books." From their unnatural dark setting, the eyes challenged his. "You must be pretty sure of yourself, James."

"No, no. If you think about it, it's a sort of a play on words. I mean, better books than—well, than fruit machines. . . ."

"Sorry, James, that's a bit beyond me. But tell me about having a bookshop."

It was an invasion already, this use of his name as a recurrent caress. The ones after his mind did it, too. "Having a bookshop? It's quite a big subject." At least he must have got his hand away; it was taking a potato crisp out of a wooden bowl.

"That's all right, James, we've plenty of time."

There was no escape. Having been manoeuvred into position with an eligible local widow, the eligible widower was expected to stay put. Perhaps it was just his mood which was making Fiona seem even less endurable than the usual hostess offering.

Nevertheless, of course, he endured her. Through another two gins apiece, a visitation from his large red host to dig an elbow literally into his ribs, and on into dinner.

To do her justice, Fiona stuck with the subject of his beloved Better Books until avocado with prawns had given way to chicken *à la crème*, asking quite intelligent questions and turning his monologue into the dialogue he so much preferred when prevailed on to talk about himself.

But all the time she reminded him of the larger cats in television wildlife films, gracefully and relentlessly stalking their prey. Under the table she had slipped the foot nearest to him out of its shoe and in searching for it had encountered his ankle. Her toes were still making the sort of movement against it her fingers had made in his palm. . . . Fiona, he was already miserably certain, was going to turn out even more alarming than the norm.

Angela! he cried inwardly. *Angela!* At first because if his wife had been at the table she would have protected him. Then because the loneliness of being without her was as sharp as ever.

"James will run you home, Fiona," said his hostess casually as she poured coffee. "Won't you, James?"

"Surely. No problem. Delighted." He'd known it was coming, of course, but it still sent his heart into his shoes. "But what's happened to your car, Fiona? You're obviously a lady used to independent travel." He couldn't resist that.

"You're quite right, James." Extra-wide eyes as if he'd offered a major revelation. "I've had clutch trouble, the garage is bringing it back tomorrow."

He'd heard it so often before, in one form or another. He'd even, at one party, looked out of a cloakroom window after dinner and seen the lady of his hostess's choice trying to hide her Mini in a clump of shrubbery.

He didn't suspect Fiona of that, but the big cat image persisted, and as he helped her into her coat he was on special alert.

"Be good!" said his host at the door, laughing uproariously, stumbling on the step as James dodged aside in the nick of time.

"Are you a good boy, James?" asked Fiona in the car.

"I'm afraid so." He'd intended to chuckle in a relaxed way, but it came out as a yelp. The last two turns were tricky, with Fiona all over him.

"I don't believe you." Her perfume alone was an ordeal. "You'll come in for a nightcap, of course." As he drew up outside a pretty bungalow, she returned to her own side of the car.

"It's kind of you, Fiona—but, no, thank you. It's been a lovely evening, but—well, time to say goodnight. . . ."

"Oh, James. Poor James. You need some help, don't you?"

"I don't think so."

He got out of the car as slowly as he could manage, went round and opened her door, accompanied her up the path. With the key in her hand she raised her face to his, and he saw by the lamp over the door that she was about to try again.

"You'll stop teasing now, won't you, James?"

"Forgive me, I'm not teasing. Goodnight, Fiona."

The face twisted, he hoped forgettably. "You're a flirt, aren't you, James? A frightened flirt."

"That's not fair!"

"Sod fairness."

She had gone, the door had banged.

She was right, fairness had nothing to do with it, James thought miserably as he hunched his way back to his car. He'd done what

politeness had demanded, and because he hadn't done any more
he'd probably lost himself a few rich customers.

At least it was unlikely he would be invited to *that* house again.

As he drove home he tried to savour the small relief but was
unable to lighten his mood of loneliness and distaste even by a walk
with mongrel Heidi beside the sea.

He couldn't go on like this.

The mood was still on him when he awoke next morning, making
him regret that it was Sunday, with no shop and unlimited opportunity to brood.

Opportunity too, though, he realized as he walked slowly round
the early spring garden with Heidi at his heels, consoled despite
himself by the tremulous sunshine and the discovery of three bril-
liantly yellow aconites, to examine the idea which had flashed in
and out of his mind the night before, somewhere around the *or-
anges au kirsch.*

The idea of taking action to bring back that loving, comfortable,
protected situation which for him was marriage.

Angela! he shouted silently. *Angela!* He laid his hand on the pale
trunk of the silver birch she had planted when they came to the
house. *It would be because we were so happy.*

He could wait, of course. Endure more Fionas, more Sophies.
More felines, more puppy dogs. The Sophy he had partnered at a
dinner four or five months ago was still sending him unsolicited
copies of her love poetry, still haunting his shop. He could wait
until chance brought him someone he could—not put in Angela's
place, of course, never that, but someone who awoke in him the
utter confidence he had felt when he asked Angela to marry him.

He hadn't got much faith, though, in chance.

Not quite knowing what he was going to do, James went indoors
and slowly over to his desk, where he sat staring out at the garden,
hardly seeing Heidi rolling about on the lawn, before pulling some
scrap paper towards him and starting to write. He wrote three
lines, scrawled impatiently across them, wrote four, scribbled them
out. He was on his third bit of paper when Harry, Heidi excitedly
beside him, strolled through the open patio door.

"Good Sunday morning, James. What on earth are you doing at your desk? Oops, sorry to startle you!"

He had been so absorbed he had yelped again on an unwelcome memory of the night before, stabbing a wavering ballpoint line across the latest piece of paper.

"All right, Harry, I'm glad to see you. I was just miles away."

"On Better Books business? Or have you taken to writing poetry to poor Sophy?"

Harry cast himself into an armchair, exhibiting what to James was his most enviable trait of continuous total relaxation. In Harry, feline grace and a constant tendency to charm were attractive attributes. And had no doubt helped him into his position as one of Linton's top estate agents.

"Neither." James thought, decided he needed one confidant. It could only be Harry. "I'm writing a short piece for *The Times.*"

"From Disgusted, Linton?"

"Not for the letter pages, for the personal column or whatever they call it nowadays. I'm advertising for a wife, Harry."

"I don't believe you."

Harry didn't want to believe him, staring at James with a sort of defensive horror.

"I'm serious, I can't stand any more of these dinner parties, these women laying siege. I only just got away with it last night."

"Why get away with it? Why not take what fate offers? Though I suppose in a small place like Linton . . ."

"Life could get awkward, yes. But you know quite well that's not why I don't. I'm a married man, Harry. That's the way I'm made. It's because I miss Angela so much that I'm going to post this today."

Harry in his lithe, quick way was beside the desk, already picking up the piece of paper under which James had swept all the others.

" 'Forty-five-year-old widower,' " read Harry aloud, " 'self-employed, bookish, living in small seaside town, seeks a second happy marriage. Further information on receipt of sympathetic response.' Sympathetic? Sounds as if you want someone to be sorry for you."

"Hell, does it? I was thinking in the sense of sympathetic nerve. French *sympathique.* Striking a chord."

"Say so, then."

"Yes. I'll think of another word. Thanks, Harry."

"Then there's bookish. Will they understand?"

"The one I want to hear from will."

"All right, all right." Harry returned the piece of paper to James's waiting fingers. "I must say it's not a bad idea. Much less drastic and more fun though to go for a series of dates. 'Forty-five-year-old widower seeks woman friend'—"

"Just what this widower doesn't seek. I want a wife, Harry. And this way I might meet a woman with at least some of the qualities I could live with."

"It's only habit, you know." Harry, recovered from his shock, threw himself back into the armchair. "You've never got out of the marriage habit and I've never got into it. Although of course if Marian hadn't died . . ." Harry's cheerful face shifted dramatically into sorrowful mode, in the way James knew it must shift each time one in his long line of women friends showed a preference for matrimony. Not for the first time he wondered if over the years since his fiancée had died of leukaemia Harry had actually come to believe his own protective myth of remaining faithful to her memory. Whether he did or not it was a stroke of public relations genius, securing his standing in the local community as a brave, sad bachelor rather than the unscrupulous womaniser James believed him to be. Unscrupulous but fair. As he stressed regularly to James, he always told his conquests at an early stage that his allegiance to Marian was ultimately binding. Wasn't it a woman's own fault if she believed herself the exception which could break his rule?

James didn't approve of his best friend, but people were what they were; you couldn't take parts of them and reject the rest. And Angela had been fond of him.

"So you won't be feeling you're letting Angela down?"

Through his own small shock at the coincidence of his thoughts with Harry's words, James noticed a faint look of holier-than-thou in the face of the faithful fiancé. It amused him. "No." *Darling, no!* "It's a tribute to Angela, Harry, if that doesn't sound too twisted up. It's because she made me so happy, made marriage so much better than any other state. Can you see?"

"I suppose so. Good luck with it, anyway. Having brought me in at the beginning you'll keep me up to date? If one of them seems too frivolous you might even hand her over."

"I might not!" Grinning, James got up from his desk. "How about exercising Heidi, then having lunch at the Yacht Club?"

I think I am an honourable man. My beard is removable but my teeth are not. . . .

He was already at work on what he was going to say next, given the right response.

CHAPTER TWO

Eve had been dreaming that Rodney still lay beside her, although behind the dream she knew he had gone.

And that he wouldn't be back.

Not that she wanted him. They'd both overreacted to that better-than-average dinner the night before, both hoped it might rekindle the mild mutual interest of their first few weeks. It had worked for the evening and the early part of the night. She'd heard him moving about the room at first light but had pretended to be asleep. He hadn't come back to the bed.

It wasn't Rodney's departure that she minded, it was the space he was leaving. The space which was the future and which his stooped, narrow shoulders had at least hidden from her the short time they'd been together. Each time a man left now, the space seemed bigger and emptier.

Well, she'd forced herself to do what she could. She'd taken a refresher course in shorthand and typing despite her announcement only a couple of years earlier that if it ever came to that she'd put her head in the oven. At least working as a temp left her free to take up the modelling offers when they came.

If they came. She was still awaiting the moment of satisfaction in which she would tell the gorgon in charge of her current office that she wouldn't be in tomorrow, Miss Griswold, she would be on a modelling assignment and she really wasn't in a position to say just when it would be over; Miss Griswold would know how it was. . . .

The room smelt frowsty and enclosed, as if the tumbled bedclothes extended over the walls and ceiling. Eve made a sudden, irritated leap out of bed towards the window, tearing the curtains apart and forcing the transom wider. A small group of women stood gossiping on the pavement outside the greengrocers opposite. The owner of the betting shop next door was just opening up. She envied them all because they were free, unimprisoned in the small, anxious cage which was Eve Harris.

The light this morning was bright and harsh, and on her way from the window she forced herself to stop at the long, cruel slope of her cheval glass. As hard on herself as the light, she wrenched her nightie over her head and flung it at the bed, but the glamour was still just there, the pout of her lips and breasts, the lustre of her red-gold hair, the length of her legs still just more noticeable than the blurring chin line and the puffy dark under her beautiful eyes. At least she could never end up a faded beauty, unnoticed; she would pass into caricature and men would continue to look at her. And award her marks for gallantry.

Eve turned away from the mirror on a sob, not so much for Rodney as at the loss of one more prop, the taking of one more step towards that widening and deepening emptiness.

The speediest antidote for depression was anger, and as her damp eyes fell on the wastepaper basket, anger flooded bracingly through her. There as usual, even on his very last visit, Rodney had left his copy of yesterday's *Times* sticking neatly up. At least he hadn't spent a quarter of an hour or so on the crossword before bed as he usually did, but he hadn't shown the rudimentary delicacy of taking the paper, this time, away with him. And the stupid part of it was that Eve was so much better at the *Times* crossword than he was. She'd leaned over him once or twice in the early days and pointed out the solution to a clue, but he had been so disturbed that after two or three nights of trying to share his habit she had disappeared into kitchen or bathroom while he struggled. He guarded the wretched square so jealously she had never discovered whether he arrived with some of it done or whether he approached it fresh on her sofa. Well, now she would be able to find out.

Suddenly shivering, Eve shrugged into a dressing gown, then ungently grabbed the paper. As she'd suspected, a very few clues had been filled in. Three clues in fact, and she had little doubt they represented the fruit of a lunch hour's effort. There was no particular cleverness, Eve thought, in being able to do crossword puzzles, it was just a quirk of mind. Rodney's dimness showed in his not being able to recognize that he didn't have it.

Squatting on the floor, she solved a couple more clues in her head before her anger turned suddenly to rage and she found herself tearing wildly at the pages, ripping them into strips and flinging them towards the ceiling. As they floated down again her fury intensified, and she began crumpling the strips into balls, giving them the impetus of small missiles which she threw about the room. When there was nothing left to rip she collapsed in tears and lay sobbing until the anger had ebbed.

Leaving absolutely nothing, at least for the precarious moment, in its place.

Cautiously, as if testing a sensitive nerve, Eve rose to her knees and crept about the room, dragging the wastepaper basket after her and putting the various shapes of paper into it as she moved around. One of the strips, comparatively unmutilated, had travelled further than the rest and landed under the window. It was the last piece of debris, and, as she stopped beside it, pressing down the rest of her collection to make room, she saw the word ANNOUNCEMENTS in bold type and found herself reading down.

Forty-five-year-old widower, self-employed, bookish, living in small seaside town, seeks a second happy marriage.
Further information on receipt of right response. Write to Box K94.

Eve didn't read any more; she scrambled to her feet a changed woman, hope surging through her more bracingly even than the rage.

All right, this particular forty-five-year-old widower might not consider her response the right one, and if he did she might hate the sight of him, but his little paragraph had showed her the answer to that gaping space.

Marriage.

Not, of course, the sort of marriage she'd contracted at the age of seventeen, going in one drastic week from the world of suburb and grammar school to the seedy edge of the law on the seedy edge of south London so as to hold on to the undreamed-of sensations experienced on her parents' bed the first time they left her on her own for a night. That marriage had been the edge of the slippery slope her mother had warned her regularly against falling over, but by the time she was legally extricated it had somehow been too late to climb back.

Promising, but must guard against an unstable streak. Eve's headmistress had said that, in a report sent to her parents only a week before she'd left their world behind her. If they'd taken note, perhaps at this moment she'd be with the sort of husband she was about to start looking for. A lawyer, perhaps—the headmistress had wanted her to go in for law.

In a way, of course, she had, helping Don keep the right side of it.

Eve laughed aloud, but partly to hide the ache which always came when she imagined how life might have been if she hadn't met Don.

An unstable streak.

Even if she hadn't met him, as she was then she would have escaped some way. Or disgraced herself and been exiled. She couldn't have conformed.

But now . . .

Self-employed, bookish, living in small seaside town . . .

She liked the sea, and she'd been bookish once, she knew what he meant. Despite the shape of her life to date she'd come to realize that she preferred men of sensitivity to what she called blokes, the machos. This forty-five-year-old widower was sensitive.

Her grammar school was a long way behind her, but it would still help her compose the right sort of letter. And in the photograph stakes she'd be miles ahead of the others even with one of her most demure . . .

The others. Absurdly, the emotion racing through her now was jealousy. But she'd show them! And if it didn't work—while she was waiting for it to work—she'd find a reputable marriage agency and register with it. Security. Prosperity. The future cosily mapped out.

Already her new and unfamiliar watchwords felt as if they'd been guarding her for years. She'd compose her response at the office, tell Miss Griswold it was something confidential their boss had asked her to do, upsetting her and with luck blunting her edge for the time it took to get her answer into an envelope. And at the office there would be Brenda—self-contained, clever, talking, when

she did, always to the point. She'd get Brenda to vet the letter, and
when it reached a stage of being approved by both of them it
would have as good a chance as any.

The little group of women had moved on to the fish shop. She
didn't envy them, their lives were so dull. The light was softening
and yellowing with sunshine; the pavement which had been shiny
was now matt. It could be a nice day. And if she didn't hurry she'd
be late for work. Which would be silly. As she wouldn't be working
forever she might as well keep Miss Griswold sweet for the time it
took to find a husband. She could put up with her now that she
knew the word *temporary* really meant what it said.

"All right, Sally?"

"Fine. Why?"

"You just seem a bit quiet."

"I'm just looking at the pictures. All right?"

"Keep your hair on, sweetie, I'm only wanting you to enjoy yourself."

"I am enjoying myself, Geoffrey. It was very kind of you to bring
us to an art exhibition when you're not really all that fond of art."

"Not fond of art! What gave you that idea? I love art!"

The rosy face beside her flamed redder in indignation. Geoffrey
was fond of art according to his own definition, Sally realized
tiredly. A chocolate-box lid over the mantlepiece, a Canaletto repro
in the hall.

"I only meant . . . I thought you might find Surrealism a bit—
confusing."

"Oh, it's rubbish really, of course," said Geoffrey with airy confidence. "A big con. No one admitting to it. But at least these fellows
could paint, which is more than can be said for most of the others."

"If I were you, Geoffrey, I should talk a bit more quietly. It's
rather bad manners to be critical so loudly."

"Sure you wouldn't rather I went home?"

"Of course not." Oh, if only he would! If only she were free to
wander, striking up conversations in mutual humility and respect
for what hung on the walls! "I just think it would be more polite to
save your criticism for when we're on our own."

For when they were sitting over dinner at the usual table in the usual restaurant, with Sally become a fluent talker in order to keep herself amused. Why on earth did she bother?

Because, she supposed, she didn't want to spend all her evenings alone or with a girlfriend, and Geoffrey was kind and so much easier to cope with than the macho sort. He protested from time to time at not being allowed to stay beyond a drink or a coffee when he brought her home, but he was easily managed. Much more easily than the sort of man she'd met at a dinner party a couple of nights ago, who had laid siege to her from the moment their hostess had introduced them. She'd enjoyed telling him she had her own car, but he'd followed her home and asked her so humbly for another coffee, a few moments in which he could be himself, she'd let him in on the strength of his initiative and his credentials as a friend of their hostess. And on a crazy moment of finding him and his appeal attractive and looking forward less than usual to her empty house. Conversation over the coffee had gone on just long enough for her to realize that once again there was no real point of contact, and then he was showing her he'd taken her gesture as a coded invitation to her bedroom. He was so sure of himself that when she'd resisted she had had the element of surprise on her side and had somehow got him to the front door, where she had been forced to listen to a gross maligning of her naïveté into a form of perversion.

She had been naive, of course, stupidly so. But she had married Tom so early, and been so happy, she had never had to learn to be manwise.

But Tom had been dead now for nearly three years, and it was time she repaired her ignorance. . . .

"That's about it, isn't it? You're ready to go?"

Geoffrey must have been as aware as she was that there was another floor of pictures they hadn't climbed to, but in the circumstances she had had enough.

"Yes, I'm ready to go. I'm sorry this hasn't been your sort of painting, Geoffrey."

"Never mind, so long as you've enjoyed it. Although I must say I can't help thinking you've been brainwashed by a lot of clever promotion." His hand was on her shoulder, but he ignored her shrug of protest. "Anyway, it's not as if I paid good money for the experience. The tickets were complimentary and kicking round the office."

"It was still thoughtful of you, Geoffrey."

She was considering telling him at the end of dinner that there didn't seem much point in their continuing to meet, but by the time dinner was over she was too tired. Anyway, she didn't really owe him any more than termination by telephone, which would be so much easier.

"You *are* quiet tonight," said Geoffrey as he drew up outside her house. "I think you're tired. Couldn't I come in and superintend a nap?"

It was the nicest side of him, and for an absurd moment she was tempted by the thought of sleeping, and waking, with a kind man beside her.

"You're a dear sometimes, Geoffrey, but no. You're right, I *am* tired, and I'm sorry if I've been crotchety this evening. But I don't feel like any company at all tonight, not even the friendly kind."

There was more than friendliness, of course, hovering on his slightly trembling mouth. Poor Geoffrey. He'd make a wonderful husband for someone who wasn't Sally Graham.

I am me! thought Sally fiercely as she trailed upstairs. *Tom knew me, and now there is nobody in the world who does.*

Not even her daughter Gill. Not in the way Tom had known her.

And there was nobody in the world she knew as she had known Tom.

Some of the loneliness was just habit, of course. Nearly half her life, the better half, had been spent with Tom, and she still wasn't used to being alone.

At least the cat was on her bed. One thing, thought Sally as she peeled off her clothes, she had learned from three years of widowhood. That the second-best to a good relationship was no relationship at all. She'd had no real happiness, no assuagement of her loneliness, from the men she had gone out with since Tom's death. Sally-and-Tom had set too high a standard.

The standard of her daily life had dropped, too. Tom had died so young and so suddenly, in mid-career and mid-mortgage, she hadn't been able to carry on the luxury of teaching art to adult people who wanted to learn, three mornings and two afternoons a week. She'd had to take a Dip. Ed. and then apply for a job as a full-time teacher in the local comprehensive, and she'd been lucky to get it.

At least Gill had been safely launched and was forging happily ahead in London at her publishing office. And at least, with the full-time job, Sally had just been able to keep her house.

What was the point, though, of her struggle? It would never make her happy. Never bring Tom back.

Tom was dead, but there had to be another man somewhere who could love and understand her and be loved and understood.

Winded by the concept, Sally walked like a zombie into the bathroom and stood before her long mirror. Blessed with a high metabolic rate, she had maintained the slightness and slimness of her youth, and her body still looked young and strong. The face above it scarcely jarred, and her fair hair was unfaded; she could be a good few years younger than forty-two. Not that the man she was looking for would judge her by her body, but it was by her body he was likely to be first attracted. . . . The words *looking for* made her wince, but the idea was expanding despite her, she was even, putting on a dressing gown as she walked, going down into the sitting room to find the day's copy of *The Times*. It was ages since she'd looked at the Personal Column, or whatever it called itself these days, but that was the place where the marriage agencies would advertise.

Tom! For the first time since he had died he didn't seem to be close at hand. Had he sensed a betrayal? But it wouldn't be that, it would be an admission that only a good husband made a good life possible.

Sally collected a pair of scissors from her desk before squatting on the floor and spreading the paper out on the carpet in front of her. On the page with the small ads she found three marriage agency advertisements, one under another, and cut out the block, her eyes drifting up the column to the word ANNOUNCEMENTS at the top. Then sharply down again.

Forty-five-year-old widower, self-employed, bookish, living in small seaside town, seeks a second happy marriage. Further information on receipt of right response. Write to Box K94.

She was really too tired to do anything that night—and anyway the marriage agency ads needed weighing up before she settled for one of them—but Sally went over to her desk and found writing paper and an envelope.

Then sat silently appealing to Tom, explaining to him why for the first time in her adult life she felt happier because of something which had nothing to do with him.

But it had everything to do with him. She was sitting as she was now, a pen in her hand, because life with Tom had been the only life worth living.

Sally put the pen to the paper and wrote a very short note to Box K94, saying that it might be agreeable for them to meet.

CHAPTER THREE

James had invited his half sister Hilda and her son Cyril for seven o'clock. As usual they arrived five minutes early.

"Cooking smells," stated Hilda in the hall as James helped her out of her coat. "You aren't using that sweetpea-scented aerosol I gave you, James."

"Sorry, sister mine. It's getting into the way of it. But they're good smells, aren't they? How are things, Cyril?"

"Busy. Very busy." Cyril rubbed his hands. It would take him about thirty years, reflected James, to grow into the age group whose mannerisms he had already adopted.

"Can't be bad." Speaking off the top of his head, James turned to lead the way into the sitting room, but Hilda had marched ahead and was already at the patio door.

"Garden looks pretty shipshape," she conceded, offering him her rare ferocious smile.

"Michael does a good job. He's like a horse in blinkers, nothing distracts him."

"He gives me the shivers," complained Cyril in his thin, rather high-pitched voice, offering fastidious illustration. "I mean . . . He's not absolutely all right, is he, James?"

"Not absolutely, no. He's a bit withdrawn. I always imagine it was something nasty he once saw in the woodshed, rather than anything actually wrong with him. But I don't know. I only know he's a jolly good gardener."

"You're very fortunate, James," said Hilda severely, sitting down where she always sat now, in Angela's chair. "And having his mother to look after you."

"I know." It annoyed James to hear himself apologetic, playing the role Hilda so often assigned to him. He went across to the drinks cupboard. "I'm cooking tonight. Lamb. Claret. What will you have now, Hilda?"

"My pale cream."

"Of course." He kept a bottle going especially for her, but always offered her the chance to make a different choice. Nothing, though, was ever different about these evenings. Except once three years ago, when Angela suddenly wasn't there to protect him through them. "Cyril?"

"I think I might venture an amontillado, thank you, James."

Cyril always "ventured" his drinks. Even a half pint—for Cyril it was always a half pint—in a pub.

"Coming up." He handed over the glasses. "Now I'll have to leave you for a moment."

James took his gin out with him to the kitchen, took his time there.

"You should let Mrs. Moxon do the dinner when you have company," said Hilda as he eventually came back. "It's more appropriate, and after a working day you deserve it." A bare ten seconds of nonresponse evoked one of her heavy sighs. "And talking of working days . . . This afternoon I was chairing a very difficult committee. I encountered a wilful obstructiveness born of an ignorance certain people have no intention of correcting. It took all my powers of persuasion."

James sat down. His nephew as usual was occupying an extreme corner of the sofa. "I can imagine."

A suspicious look. "It wasn't easy. I had virtually no support."

Everybody out of step but Johnny. "The opposition didn't have a point?"

"On the contrary, they had a large number. Every one of them totally misguided."

Hilda's mouth told her story, reflected James for the umpteenth time. Small, thin, pursed. Not their father's mouth, and their father had been open and generous to the point of stupidity. Hilda's mother he knew only from photographs, but he had once taken a magnifying glass to her sepia lips and seen Hilda on the rare occasions she was anxious to please.

"But they saw it your way eventually, Hilda?"

"Enough of them."

"You are marvellous, Mummy," said Cyril.

"The meal's ready, actually," said James, ready himself for the next break. "If you'd like to go through I'll bring it in."

They always refused a second drink, so he'd stopped offering one. He downed a refill of his own before taking the joint into the dining room.

Hilda as usual was in Angela's place. She'd taken it from the first time it was vacant, like the sitting-room chair. Perhaps she'd just wanted to spare him the bleakness of the empty seats, but James was still resentful that she hadn't asked.

"As it comes, Hilda?"

"No fat. A very little gravy."

"Of course."

The meat was good and she said so, enthusiastically echoed by her son. Hilda catered economically.

"So you're enjoying work in London, Cyril?"

"I should say so! The journey's tedious, though."

"You should drive in."

"Nowhere to leave the car."

No, of course not, only partners if not senior partners would merit a company car space in the city. "The time will come," James prophesied with reluctant confidence.

"He's getting on very well," observed Hilda, "but they take advantage of him."

"Oh?"

"Yes, they keep him so late in the evenings. It can be ten or eleven o'clock before he's home."

"Too bad, Cyril." James expected either complacency or resentment in the young–old face but saw embarrassment, and pale eyes sliding down to the table. Something suddenly told him that if he telephoned the offices of Charnock, Ellis and Jones at seven o'clock one evening, it would be unlikely to be his nephew who answered. Well, he couldn't blame Cyril; cleverer men than he would have found it impossible to lead a private life under Hilda's gimlet gaze. So why didn't the fellow get his own place?

Because, James answered himself, Cyril was too fond of the ease and comfort which went with his mother's domination. Not a young man he had much regard for. Which was a pity. With his own son somewhere along the remoter reaches of the Amazon, it could have been fun to have a nephew at hand.

"You're very quiet, James."

"Am I, Hilda? I'm sorry. But we ought to have reached a stage by now, don't you think, where we have no need to make conversation?"

"There are silences and silences," rebuked Hilda mysteriously.

"Oh, but that's true. More meat?"

The offer was declined by both mother and son, and the opportunity rendered of pulling a couple of Lucky Jim faces in the kitchen while he deposited the dishes and assembled the pudding. Sometimes James felt an absurd sense of guilt that he hadn't succeeded in making at least something of Hilda and Cyril, however uphill the task.

It was a relief when, towards the end of•the *charlotte russe,* Harry put his head round the dining-room door.

"Oops!" said Harry. "I didn't know you were having company. Good evening, Hilda. Cyril."

"Good evening, Harry." Hilda's ferocious smile was on her again. She liked Harry. Cyril looked apprehensive. Slightly more sensitive than his mother, he knew Harry to be beyond them both.

"We're just going through for coffee," said James thankfully. "I'll include you."

Out in the kitchen his relief turned suddenly and sickeningly to alarm. He hadn't told Hilda about his *Times* notice, and she was the last person in the world he wanted to know about it. But he'd been so open about the business with Harry, Harry might take it Hilda knew, too, and mention it. He might have mentioned it already.

James almost fell into the sitting room with the coffee tray, but Hilda's face told him the worst had happened.

"Harry has been telling me something very peculiar, James. I thought at first it was a joke, but he assures me it isn't."

"Sorry," muttered Harry, looking uncomfortable for the first time James could remember.

"And what has Harry been telling you, Hilda?"

"I can scarcely put it into words. He tells me you've—that you've actually *advertised*—in *The Times*—for a *wife!*"

"Would you sooner I'd advertised in the *Mirror* for a baboon?"
The only thing now was to go on the offensive. Certainly not be
apologetic. And he didn't feel apologetic, which was exhilarating.

"There's no need to be rude, James." How often she'd said that,
in just that way, during his nursery days, the plain girl in her early
teens looking down aghast at the unfortunate fact of a younger
brother! Now she was looking up at him, craning her arthritic neck
as he stood tall and smiling beside her chair. There was no need to
let her upset him.

"Sorry, but you talk to me as if I was younger than Cyril. I'm a
middle-aged man who's had a very happy marriage. Followed by
three far less happy years as a widower. Now I'd like another
happy marriage." He didn't have to justify himself to Hilda, for
heaven's sake. But he was going on. "As those three years have
failed to offer me anyone I consider remotely appropriate, I've
decided to approach the matter direct. I would have thought the
simplicity of it would have appealed to you, sister mine."

She had flushed, and Cyril's putty-coloured face was now pink.

"There are so many decent women in Linton . . ." It was
Hilda's only feeble remark of the evening, and the way she broke
off and angrily shook her head showed that she knew it.

"Are there? Whether or not, this is what I've decided to do."

And, crossing to his desk, he'd decided to give her the works.
"This is the Xeroxed CV I sent out, Hilda, in each case with a
short personal note. There were six replies, four of them possibles,
so the CV went out four times, with a photograph. So far I've had
three responses in kind."

He laid the pile in her lap, hearing Harry's appreciative murmur.

"James! I've no wish to know the sordid details!" Nevertheless,
of course, she was reading.

"Sordid? Come, come, Hilda. The details might be sordid if I'd
approached some dating outfit." He and Harry exchanged looks.
"This was a straightforward request for a wife, for someone who
might share my interests, understand my temperament, and live
with me for the rest of my days. I'm not looking for a call girl, for
heaven's sake!"

"No? What's this, then?"

Triumphantly Hilda brandished the photograph she had

snatched from under the clip holding one series of papers. "'Eve Harris,'" she read from the top sheet. "'Mizz.' Well, that speaks for itself."

"Not necessarily these days, Mummy . . ." began Cyril diffidently.

With a wave of the photograph Hilda swept her son aside. "If this—lady—is seeking marriage, James, I'm—I'm a Hottentot."

"It appears she is. She's written a very good letter. Read it, Hilda."

"Anyone can write a good letter. You're a fool, James."

"In your opinion. Which in this instance doesn't count." He could feel the pulse in his temple; he was going to have to work to keep his calm. But it would be worth it; he had far more real power to annoy Hilda than she to annoy him, the mainstay of which was to appear totally undisturbed by whatever she said. He would be a fool in his own opinion, too, if he threw away that prime advantage. "Don't worry, Hilda," he went on, managing a smile. "I've plenty of common sense and I won't do anything I'll regret. All I'm intending to do at the moment so far as Ms. Harris is concerned is take her out to dinner. Likewise the others."

Harry had made one of his lithe movements across the room and taken the photograph from the arm of Hilda's chair where she had thrown it down. James watched the absorption of his face as he studied it, then saw him glance across at Cyril, whose furtively eager eyes were moving between his mother and Harry's hand. As Hilda lowered her head again to the papers, the hand shot sideways like the elastic front paw of a cat and deposited the photograph on the arm of the sofa. James looked away in distaste as his nephew's neat head struggled for a position from which to study the photograph without the gesture of the hands which might secure his mother's unwanted attention.

"*Any* of these women, James," Hilda was continuing, rapping the pile in her lap, "might be—well, they might be *drug traffickers,* or—or international criminals hoping to get you innocently involved."

"Hilda!"

She had dropped her eyes again to the pile, knowing she had gone over the top. Cyril quickly moved the photograph on the sofa arm to ease the angle of his neck.

"James!" Again Hilda was blazing at him, and seeing what she now held in her hand he knew that this time she felt on surer ground. "To send your whole history—*yourself*—out into the blue, to four women you've never met! It's—well, it's very unwise, of course, but apart from that it's—it's so vulgar!"

Harry, relaxed again and enjoying himself, was looking from one sibling to the other and back again under lowered lids. Cyril was still studying the photograph on the arm of the sofa.

"You made it sound quite romantic, Hilda," managed James with a savage effort of self-control. "Until you said, 'vulgar.' I seem to remember your telling me, not once but many times, that 'vulgar' is what one is, not what one does."

"I don't know what I'm saying tonight, James, you've upset me so much. If mother had lived to learn—"

"She would undoubtedly have been horrified. Mine would have understood." It was as unkind as he would get. "Don't waste energy on feeling shocked, Hilda. I have dinner dates with four women, or soon will have. That's all. No obligation on either side for more than that. And I don't really think there's anything on that sheet of paper to interest a KGB agent."

"It's common!" said Hilda decisively. "Whatever you say, James, it's common."

"So is the behaviour of some of the ladies of Linton I'm invited to meet at dinner parties. Cheer up, Hilda. It doesn't affect you or Cyril, and no one outside this room need know about it if you don't choose to tell them."

"I certainly don't choose, James! And I hope I'm speaking for Harry!"

It was an illustration of her confidence in her power over Cyril, reflected James, that she didn't so much as glance warningly in his direction. She sought and received from Harry an unnaturally solemn assurance that he would conceal James's aberration from their mutual acquaintances. "That particular photograph, Harry," she pursued. "I mean, it sums it all up. Do you think it's the photograph of a woman who wants to get *married?* Have another look at it. Cyril!"

Picking the photograph up, Cyril had pushed his luck. With a guilty start he fumbled it into Harry's outstretched hand. Harry stared at it thoughtfully while Cyril tried to avoid his mother's outraged stare.

"She looks more game for a date than eager to become a wife," said Harry at last, judicially. "But as James said, you never can tell, and there's only one way to find out."

"I beg your pardon?" boomed Hilda.

"By meeting her, of course." Harry leaned back in his chair, smiling at Hilda. "James may be doing something you consider common, Hilda, but he does have the nous to sniff out the phony when encountered face to face. I really shouldn't worry."

"I *do* worry, though," protested Hilda. But the fire was going out of her. "Not that it means anything to James. He was always independent."

James caught Cyril's envious sideways look and felt his first pang of pity for the boy. Hilda, after all, was only his elder sister. To have her for a mother would be a grave handicap to the strongest of sons.

"This time next year, Hilda," said James, "you'll be telling me the woman sitting in your chair"—it was his parting shot—"is the second best thing that ever happened to me."

"Don't be silly, James." Hilda got to her feet. It was almost her usual departure time, but it could just be that his mention of the chair had made her uneasy. "Come along, Cyril, it's time we were going."

"Yes, Mummy. Goodbye, James. Thanks for a nice evening."

"A somewhat unusual one, perhaps," said James, trying to make Hilda smile at him. And discovering with a qualm that although it was true he didn't care what she thought of his enterprise, she had somehow managed to transmit to him a sense of unease.

After they'd gone he didn't tell Harry about it; Harry would only say it served him right for trying to tie himself up again legally. When Harry, too, had gone it took a long walk by the sea with Heidi before he felt strong enough to tackle the remains of dinner. Then a long time in the sitting room with a book on his knee he wasn't reading, before he was able to go to bed.

CHAPTER FOUR

The day James's letter came, Sally left home before the postman's early visit. She had promised a private half hour to one of her best pupils, tearfully on her way through a stagnant patch, and as the young headmaster was a relentless theorist who disapproved of what he called "teacher's petism," it seemed prudent to meet the girl before his arrival at school precisely in time to preside over assembly.

The rescue operation in the cold studio turned out to be the one agreeable event of that working day. Immediately after assembly she was summoned to the headmaster's office and presented with the latest in a series of blueprints aimed at "structuring" her teaching of art. Or art studies, as he preferred to call it. Sally had evidence that he didn't know a Rembrandt from a Rubens and resented his interference, but no member of staff was allowed to escape regular exposure to the headmaster's educational experiments, and so she swallowed her annoyance and agreed to put his new theory into practice. Mid-morning he came to the studio to watch, staying just long enough to witness her failure.

"I appreciate it's difficult to climb out of a groove, Mrs. Graham, and face the modern way." He had paused by the door, far enough away from her to have to raise his voice. "But just keep trying."

It was inexcusable to brand her a fuddy-duddy in front of her pupils; it broke the first rule of loyalty. And he had made no allowance for self-consciousness, or the intractable nature of his new material. Sally was so indignant it was several moments before she could appreciate that her class was on her side, mimicking his mannerisms and making futile but touching suggestions for strike action.

Left to herself, Sally saw her art classes as oases in her life as a schoolteacher, but in the wake of one of the headmaster's theories these tended to dry up, and the rest of the day in the studio was as much of a struggle as the hours spent outside it. Even a free period in which she'd hoped to do some painting on her own account was hijacked for the invigilation of the school's most unruly class, sitting a maths test which had been the parting shot of a teacher on the way down with flu. Although from the start of her enforced new career Sally had found herself able to maintain discipline, it was at a cost to nerves and stamina.

At ten to four one of the tinies was sick, and Sally the only member of staff who appeared to have the time to run her home. The child produced a key to an empty house, and Sally put her to bed, waited an hour for the mother, then sat with her for another hour over a pot of tea trying to be tactfully disapproving. When she eventually got home she was tired and cross.

On the floor behind her front door were an obvious junk package and a letter addressed in handwriting she didn't recognize. Since posting her note to Box K94 Sally had lived in an aura of self-disapproval, but she stared at the unknown writing for several seconds without connecting it with her new frame of mind. She had the envelope open, was looking at a photograph of a handsome, half-smiling, bearded man, before realizing what she had in her hands.

Then, her legs trembling, she sat down to read it.

The handwritten note first, agreeing with her it would be pleasant to have dinner, offering her the alternatives of London or—seeing she didn't live there—the seaside town which was the writer's home. *We have one very good hotel, the Grand, where I propose we meet if you prefer to come down here. Should you wish to stay overnight I can recommend the accommodation, but of course that is up to you. I apologize that the attached curriculum vitae should be photocopied, but to my surprise I have received several replies to my notice!* Civilized, relaxed, self-deprecating.

The CV confirmed the favourable impression, painting the picture of a modest, humorous and educated man.

A real man?

Or a PR job?

Sally stared at the photograph, finding it as ultimately unreadable as the letter and the CV, not only because of the beard. But at least the eyes as well as the mouth seemed to be smiling.

Jumping to her feet, Sally transferred the contents of the envelope to her desk and went to feed the cat. She made herself wait until she'd completed a drawing and had supper before going to her desk again.

Then she stared for moments at the photograph, reread the CV and the letter, found herself at the same time exhilarated and cast down. How was she to match the highly favourable impression created on her by the already legendary James Edward Marshall?

After a few doodling moments trying to be clever she decided it must at least be simply. And honestly. By saying how happy she'd been with Tom and how much she'd preferred teaching art to adults for ten hours a week than art, English, history and French to schoolchildren for thirty-five. By telling him about Gill and her painting and liking animals and the theatre and old films. She wrote through a depressed conviction of the bald ordinariness of what she was putting down, but when she read it over she thought perhaps a hint of personality came through. Enough to keep him from regretting his invitation to dinner? In her covering note accepting the invitation she offered him a way out. . . . *If it still stands after you've had a look at the enclosed!*

The letter asked her to suggest a couple of dates, as well as choose the rendezvous, and she offered two close together a fortnight ahead, when the spring term would have ended. After looking up Linton on the map she chose the seaside rather than London. If he wrote back confirming one of the dates she'd turn her enterprise into the short break she'd already decided to give herself during the Easter holidays. But she wouldn't contact the Grand Hotel unless and until he did confirm—both dates could already have been promised to other women who had responded to his *Times* notice. *Tom, I am in a line of women queuing up for a man.* If he did still want to meet her she'd book a room for three or four nights. Without of course telling him, either in advance or when they were together. . . .

When they were together? Despite the excellent impression created by the papers under her hand it was still impossible to think of James Edward Marshall as a real person. Almost impossible, since she had embarked on this outrageous exercise, to think of herself as one. But the problem of her own identity had begun, of course, after the death of Tom. Was there enough of her left to choose or be chosen?

Well, she was about to find out. And if there wasn't, then at least she might get Tom back.

Tearing out to the tube with the extra reluctance of a Monday morning, Eve met the postman on the stairs.

"Nothing for me as usual?"

But her voice had asked a question, and the postman answered it with a long envelope addressed strongly and unfamiliarly by hand.

"Thanks!"

Without the clear postmark she would still have known. Eve stuffed the envelope deep into her bag, glad the press of bodies on the rush hour underground would save her from the temptation to open it unsuitably in public and reveal to swivel eyes the inevitable mixture of business and intimacy it was bound to contain.

She knew too, as soon as she burst into her office, that it was her lucky day.

"Hi." Brenda looked up from her desk in her usual lazy way. "No need to bother trying to look as if you've been here for hours. Griswold's had to go to the dentist."

"Oh, Brenda! So how much grace do we have?"

"Mr. Smith tells me she couldn't get an appointment till ten, and that he just managed to persuade her not to come in for half an hour at nine. Such devotion! I should say we've two hours at least."

"What marvellous timing. Brenda, I've something to show you. It's come, the letter from wonder man."

"Well, good."

How contained she was, thought Eve, trying as she scrabbled in her bag not to feel checked by Brenda's cool. Sitting there so neat and narrow in her plain dark clothes, her straight dark hair cut over the weekend so that her quizzically poised head looked even smaller on her long, pale neck than it had looked on Friday. No beauty—her pale features somehow too economical, her lips just too thin, her eyes set too deep—but what style, what self-possession! Not from being pleased with herself, which Eve would have laughed at instead of reluctantly envying. Rather, Eve always thought, from a sort of laziness. As if it didn't matter. As if she was all right as she was, not having to bother to make an impression, sing for her supper. If Brenda's temperament had been different she'd have been in Miss Griswold's place. Or somewhere much better. But Brenda saw no reason to make the effort.

"I haven't opened it yet. I'm going to open it now."

"I'm privileged." Brenda wasn't really being sarcastic, leaning her elbows on her desk and her chin on her hands she was as intrigued as she ever was over anything, as intrigued as she'd been when Eve had composed her own CV and covering letter, offering a better choice of word, a more precise turn of phrase, until they had both pronounced the effort as good as it could be.

Nevertheless Eve's heart was pounding, her fingers were clumsy as she poked about with the point of the paper-knife.

"I expect he's got fixed up," she said aloud, to preempt disappointment. She'd got the contents out but the envelope was devastated. "Oh, Brenda!" There was a handwritten note on top. James Marshall had been pleased to receive her photograph and CV and would be happy if she would have dinner with him. " 'If you still think this a good idea after you've studied the enclosed!' He's modest with it, Brenda, I like that."

"It's unusual in a man."

"You can say that again. Have a look at the photo."

It was Eve who got up and carried it across the space between them.

"Hm, not bad. But neither are you."

"I'm over the hill." But praise from Brenda, delivered in the same precise, unenthusiastic voice she used for everything, was praise indeed. "Thanks, though, I could do with a boost. Especially now that Rodney's packed up."

"Good riddance, from all you've told me."

"Well, yes . . ."

"You didn't want him."

"No . . ."

"You were always saying how impossible he was."

"Well, yes . . . Even so . . ."

"You'll feel the gap."

"Well, yes . . . But not just that," went on Eve insincerely, thinking more about Brenda. Was there a gap in Brenda's life, and if so, did she feel it?

Not for the first time Eve was aware of annoyance with the bad bargain she entered into daily with Brenda. Giving everything, receiving nothing. Brenda knew all about her marriage and her modelling career and that extraordinary ex-king she'd met in Spain and as many of her other boyfriends as had left a memory. All she knew about Brenda was that she spoke good French and had a brother. But when she asked Brenda questions she somehow didn't get an answer. She didn't know whether Brenda had a boyfriend or even a girlfriend, whether she told things to someone else or didn't need to tell things to anyone. There were people like that, of course, there must be, but Brenda was the only one she'd known personally. It had its advantages, of course: Brenda wasn't waiting all the time to get her own oar in like other women Eve had known, who never really listened because they were working out what they were going to say themselves. Brenda at least listened; there was evidence of that in the way she came out with things she'd remembered—things sometimes which Eve herself had forgotten she'd said until Brenda reminded her. And if asked, Brenda was nearly always prepared to give her opinion. In fact, she was probably the best kind of a person to have around just now.

"Go on, Eve, you're not going to miss Rodney!"

"Well, perhaps not if I get to know this James. It has left a gap, you know. He sounds pretty super, doesn't he, Brenda?"

Brenda laid the photograph down.

"He sounds too good to be true, but I suspect he might just be the way he sounds. But for goodness' sake take care of yourself, Eve. And be prepared for disappointment. On both sides."

"I know, I know. And there's always the marriage agencies. I intend to register with one."

"Very wise."

"If I still need to after I've met James."

"Only then, of course." Brenda yawned and stretched, reminding Eve of a lean black cat.

"Why don't you register with a marriage agency yourself,

Brenda? Though I suppose that brother of yours must introduce you to men from time to time."

Eve was aghast at herself as soon as she'd spoken, but Brenda was smiling. "I don't meet Malcolm's friends, and I'm too lazy to take any initiatives." *I'm all right as I am,* interpreted Eve. "Your acceptance of the dinner invitation won't pose any problems." She hadn't so much as given Brenda food for thought. "You've written the hard part. But when you meet him, Eve . . . try to play it cool."

"You think I'll go over the top?" demanded Eve aggressively, even though she knew Brenda was trying to help her. And that was just what she might do.

"I think there's a chance of it, and you'll make a better impression if you don't. Now, get your letter written while you've got the chance."

But Mr. Smith's buzzer went, and it appeared Brenda was busy. By the time Eve came out of his office the bonus time was almost up. She had written her note of acceptance but not shown it to Brenda or prepared the envelope, when Miss Griswold appeared in the doorway.

"Good morning, Miss Griswold. How are you feeling?" Brenda spoke as Eve swept her private papers out of sight.

"I shall be all right." But Miss Griswold's face was assymetrical, and her edge for the time being was blunted. When she left them, on a comparatively feeble injunction to get on with their work, Eve had the courage to show her note to Brenda, write the envelope, and stamp it. Then when her lunch hour came all she had to do was to push it into the letter box outside the sandwich bar.

CHAPTER FIVE

"All right, Dusty, ten thousand. And that's my last word."

"All right, Mr. Newbury." The voice at the other end, raised against the surrounding cacophony of the betting shop, sounded elaborately injured. "Ten thousand it is."

"In cash, Dusty. In the morning."

"All right, all right. Now I've gotter go."

"I wouldn't dream of detaining you a moment longer than necessary. It isn't necessary, is it? *Hell!*"

"Mr. Newbury? I told you, you'll have the money in the morning—"

"It's all right, Dusty. Minor disaster this end. Cheers."

Cursing in more detail, Malcolm dropped the receiver onto its cradle, righted the tumbler rolling on the edge of the leather-topped table, and sped to the kitchen for a cloth.

A funny way to be, he thought as he mopped at the golden spill lengthening across his fawn carpet, *lazy and fussy at the same time.* He went back a couple of times to rinse out the cloth and bring it through for another application. The third time he brought kitchen paper and spread it over the damp to absorb it. With luck there wouldn't be a stain—whisky neat wasn't like red wine or those awful sticky mixers.

One of the reasons he liked going to Brenda's was the way his fussiness dropped off him the moment he was through her front door, letting his coat fall on the floor behind him and having to be reminded to wipe his feet as she picked it up. Being at Brenda's was a sort of throwback, he supposed, to being in their childhood home, where it had never crossed his mind to clear up after himself. Now that he thought about it, he could still see his mother's face when she had come into his bedroom once while he was in bed being lazy, and seen him eating buttered toast off the blanket.

Yet when he'd got his own place he'd found himself suddenly, pedantically, aware of his surroundings. If anyone shed a crumb or spilled a drop of liquor in the flat he was there with the dustpan or the cloth, or itching to be there if it really wasn't on at that moment for him to run for them. Like the other night when Tracy had got excited and flung an arm out and knocked her glass of Pernod off the bedside table. Even at a time like that he'd wanted to jump out of bed and fetch the bathroom cloth. . . .

It was a relief to have set up that deal via Dusty. He'd be all right now for a few months, could even take a week or so off before setting up the next one. Although he probably wouldn't, his boredom threshold was so low he'd be glad after a few days to start working something else out. He hadn't been round Larry lately. He'd look Larry up and see what was doing in the used car business. Might go and call on him in the morning when he'd collected from Dusty. . . .

Malcolm slouched over to the window and stood looking out on the ugly, angular skyline, noting not for the first time that every squat, rectangular building seemed to have a small, even uglier replica clamped to its flat grey top. Enclosed liftshafts, air-conditioning plants, staircase ends, he supposed. Brenda was always telling him he ought to get his paints out again, but what could you do with a landscape like that? Even if he made anything of it, it was bad enough having it for real without recording it. If he could only start setting up better deals he could think about moving, although really the flat suited him well enough, it was easy to run and had everything he needed. And on the river side, the side where he had no windows, things were looking up, they were developing dockland and even this dreadful building would have to increase in value. Best to hang on.

Another advantage was neighbours as indifferent to the community around them as he was himself. If he moved to a more salubrious spot he might have lonely housewives knocking at his door to borrow sugar.

Initially the image made him shudder, but then he began to think what the lonely housewives might be like and fell into a pleasantly erotic daydream in which he kept one happy during the afternoons, and passed her husband in the road morning and evening with a formal greeting.

Pleasure without responsibility! It should be the motto on his personal coat of arms. Better in Latin, of course, but he couldn't remember any Latin beyond a few declensions of nouns and conjugations of regular verbs. In the quarters he'd have a horse, a car, a woman and a wad of money. The whole surmounted by an artist's palette to please Brenda. Painting life as it was . . .

Malcolm grimaced at his faint reflection in the window, crossed the room to the drinks cupboard and replaced the spilled whisky. Then with the glass in his hand started pacing about.

What he should have been doing earlier in the day, of course, was walking or running around the park down the road, then he wouldn't be feeling now like a caged tiger. But his high metabolic rate took care of the slim figure he was so proud of, and there was no other incentive sufficient to get him out.

He was bored, though. Perhaps Tracy was back.

Malcolm stopped in front of his armchair, flopped into it and pulled the telephone towards him, being careful to set his glass down beyond the sweep of his arm. He dialled Tracy's number and leaned back.

"Hello?" The usual mixture of hope and wariness.

"Tracy? So you're back."

"Oh, Malcolm." Only wariness, now. Something was different.

"What's up, Tracy? Someone with you?"

"No one's with me." Too quick and defensive; someone was. "I was reading."

"So you're coming out of an anaesthetic. All right. How about me coming over later?" He asked, now, only out of curiosity to see how she'd tackle it.

"Not tonight, Malcolm, I think I'm getting a chill. I'll ring you."

He watched his knuckles whiten on the handset, as if they were someone else's. Well, he'd only thought of her because just now there was no one else.

There was, though. He had a sudden sharp memory of throwing himself down on Brenda's bed as an unhappy child, and taking her old teddy bear into his arms.

"Too bad, Tracy. You better nurse it. Cheers."

He rang off and dialled Brenda's number.

"Bebe, can I come over?"

"You can come for supper, Mal."

It was as though he'd found a small fire and was warming his hands at it. She'd say that, as matter-of-factly, if she hadn't seen him for months. And in fact, now he thought of it, it was weeks since he'd rung her.

"Thanks, I will. Sorry it's been so long. I seem to have been busy."

"All to the good. I know you come when you can."

If he could have seen his sister's face he might have been able to tell whether or not she was being sarcastic. As her voice was always slightly ironic, it was impossible to tell from sound alone. Not that Bebe's face gave much away, but over a lifetime he thought he had learned to read its minimal signals.

"I've had a chill, as well. Are you feeling any better?"

"I'm all right, Mal. We'll talk when you get here."

Brenda replaced her receiver and strolled out to the kitchen. She'd been going to make do with a pizza and salad, but there were more interesting things in the freezer, and there was the microwave to thaw them out.

As she assembled some of Mal's favourite foods her face wore the faint, contented smile she seldom permitted it in public. She liked cooking for Mal. Weak Mal, ingenious Mal, familiar Mal. Mal who was always there, grinning the relief of both of them, when she came back to herself after her abortive sorties along the road to matrimony.

Several times she had thought she was going to reach it. Or, she wondered now, had she really thought so, deep down? Certainly she had gone through the motions, had even, for a few weeks, worn some man's engagement ring (she could remember the alien sensation of it on her finger, see the winking diamond in her mind's eye, but had to search for the name of the donor). But each time, when it came to the crunch, she'd had to back off.

Even with Barry.

Almost from the start she'd believed that she wanted to make it

with Barry, that this was what she'd been waiting for. Even at the
interview for the high-powered job as his personal assistant she'd
been aware of the attraction hanging between them.

But he was married, and he was a man with principles. Brenda
hadn't been in the least concerned about Barry's wife, but she had
persuaded herself that his principles were an essential part of the
man she loved, and had been content for three years to do no more
than work for him. During them she'd received an award for being
the best PA in London, and when Barry's wife left him she thought
she was ready to enter his empty arms.

Only when he opened them she found that she wasn't.

And that again she shared Mal's relief.

Wasn't the truth of it that she didn't want to get married to
anyone, didn't want to commit herself? If she'd wanted it she
couldn't have enjoyed those three years with Barry the way she had
allowed them to be, years of glances and glancings away, of exaggerated mutual respect and offices charged with suppressed emotions—the scenario which ought to have brought impatience and
frustration. She wouldn't be missing, now, merely the comfortably
ambiguous situation of believing herself in love with Barry and
being prevented by his moral scruples from having to do anything
about it. Peeling potatoes, Brenda faced the fact that she would
have been content to go on like that until she or Barry retired from
business, go on leaving Barry behind at the end of the working day
and cooking meals for Mal when he got round to visiting her.

She ought to have been a psychiatrist, she thought as she moved
about her neat kitchen; she had the power of analysis and an ability
to remain detached even from herself which sometimes almost
shocked her.

She hadn't heard from Barry now for over a month; he must
have taken it in at last that he was wasting his time. Occasionally
an unfamiliar sensation of shame swept over her that she had let
him down, but she was able to control it with the thought that
nothing had ever been said between them over those three years
which would have sounded in any way remarkable if overheard by
other members of his staff. Sometimes the sense of shame related
to her half-belief that if Barry hadn't done what was expected of
him when his wife left him—immediately asked Brenda to take her

place—she would have been as devastated as he had been by her refusal.

Intellectually. The whole thing was that she had no heart.

For a moment Brenda's step quickened about her domain as she tried to outwalk the conclusion she had been moving towards since she had turned Barry down. She didn't want to be sloppy like Eve, but she wanted to have feelings, wanted to be human and not a monster.

But Barry had suddenly looked absurd.

"Brenda . . . Darling . . . I thought we both under-stood. . . ."

His mouth had trembled, his face had looked quite different. Weak. Helpless. At least she'd been shocked that her chief sensation should be embarrassment.

"I'm sorry, Barry. We've worked exceptionally well together, and you've misunderstood it."

"I certainly have. Brenda . . . Couldn't we just see if—"

"I'm sorry, Barry."

She found she didn't even want an affair. And that she was struggling against hysterical laughter. She had, of course, been able to control it as she gave a month's notice.

It had been a terrible month, recalled Brenda as she transferred the browned meat to a casserole dish. Barry had started to remind her of a dog anxious but unable to please its master, and her own detachment had grown by the day. Her cruel detachment.

Really, she should carry a government health warning.

As she put the completed casserole into the oven Brenda laughed.

It had taken its toll, though. The flu virus she'd come down with the day after she'd left Barry's office seemed to have gone on and on and had made her thinner than ever. Mal had been especially busy and hadn't got in to see her as often as she'd hoped he would when he knew she was ill. It had taken a couple of months for her to feel well enough to think about working again.

Barry had been magnanimously full of suggestions for another permanent high-powered job, but somehow she'd wanted a breathing space, and not to see for the time being into the future. So she'd registered with an agency and taken temporary jobs which she'd been able to walk out of the moment she'd mastered them or become bored. She'd be walking out of her current one any moment now, and might already have done so if she hadn't been mildly interested in what happened to Eve. Poor vulnerable Eve, actually looking for a man to whom to surrender her independence . . .

She'd get in touch with the new City College, see if there was some sort of course to do with psychiatry, or psychoanalysis, or a related discipline. She could feel a sort of excitement coming up to take the place of the excitement of those years with Barry. Everything was going to change.

Except for her one constant. Mal.

He was only twenty minutes late and he enjoyed her dinner.

"That was great, Bebe." He had moved as usual to her larger armchair, was almost lying down in it, his long legs spread across the rug.

"I'll get the coffee."

"Don't be long." He spoke lazily, out of his utter relaxation. Pity he didn't fancy Bebe, he would have been able to keep it all in the family. The idea appealed to the neatness in him, failed to stir a moral repulsion, although there was a reflex protest in his gut. That, though, could only be because of not finding Bebe sexually attractive; he wasn't a man to be affected by a taboo.

He was glad she hadn't married. She'd have wanted to go on doing things for him, of course, but a husband would have diluted her concern merely by being there. He didn't think she'd marry now, after that latest long-drawn-out fiasco. Poor Bebe. But he shouldn't pity her, she wasn't sorry for herself.

"I've stirred and put the cream in. Don't touch it again if you want to drink the coffee through the cream."

"Thanks, Bebe. You know it all, don't you? Come and sit beside me."

Silently she dropped to the floor, leaned against his knees as he drew them up, turned her head from side to side as absently he stroked her hair. "I'm sorry it's a gas fire," she said eventually. "Remember that fire in the nursery?"

"With the guard like a zimmer with a brass top? Yes, I always wanted it to be taken away so that we could get at the heat. Mummy took it away once and I never forgot what it felt like."

"I remember. And I remember when you were sick on my teddy and Mummy washed him and put his arms through the mesh of the fireguard so that he would dry. I can still see him hanging there with the firelight on his tummy. It upset me because I thought it was undignified for him."

"I can remember that now too, I'd forgotten. I remember you sticking up for me that time Mummy said I'd run over her bloody tulip shoots. You stamped your foot at her."

"I'd seen that boy from next door trampling around. It was when you were playing hide and seek. It was the only time Mummy was unfair. You remember unfairness."

"Yes." When his mother's sorrow that he hadn't stuck out the course at art college had turned to anger he had called her unfair. But he had wasted her money, of which there hadn't been all that much after their father died. Not that that was why she'd been angry, her anger had been an extreme form of disappointment. Which he had never done anything to ease. He was the one who'd been unfair. . . .

"Time I went, Bebe, got to get up early in the morning." In the morning he'd certainly go and see Larry, go and see what was moving in the car market. If his mother hadn't died she'd have known at least that he was making a living.

"I'll just give you another cup of coffee." He didn't want one, but she was already on her feet, pouring it out. "What else d'you remember, Mal?"

CHAPTER SIX

"James? I thought I might catch you over your lunch hour." There was a note in Hilda's voice when she spoke to him on the telephone which always struck an unsympathetic chord somewhere about his middle ear.

"What is your pleasure, sister mine?"

"You sound cheerful, James. I hope it means you have abandoned that absurd idea of yours."

"Which absurd idea, Hilda?"

"You know perfectly well what I'm talking about. The idea of . . . of advertising for a wife." Hilda had lowered her voice, although James was fairly certain she was alone. It was as if she wanted to keep the full horror of his enterprise even from herself.

"On the contrary, Hilda. I have just about got the full package sewn up."

"I see." He sensed her struggle between outrage and curiosity. Curiosity won. "Does that include the woman whose photograph you showed us the other night?"

"It does indeed. In fact I'm meeting her next week. At The Poet's Restaurant in Hampstead. I have high hopes of the encounter."

"I can't believe it of you, James."

"Brace up, Hilda." On the whole he preferred his sister tart to tearful. "The first may be the last." He wasn't going to tell her that this encounter with Eve Harris would be his second. The first—in London a couple of nights ago—had been even worse than the latest dinner party. He shuddered on the memory. "If Ms. Harris and I take to one another I may decide not to bother with any of the others."

"James! This can't be you talking!"

"It's me, Hilda."

It wasn't, of course, it was the demon in him, an alien creature of breezy self-assurance which attacked when Hilda tried to push him into a corner. As she did this nearly every time they met she saw a great deal of it. Now that he thought about it, in fact, it was likely his sister knew little or nothing of his real nature; he had been trying to shock her since he was in the nursery. Sometimes he wished he had grown out of this particular childish habit, but he would probably have been unable to manage her without it.

"You've changed, James."

"I rather wish I had. Did you want to ask me something, Hilda? Apart from the progress of my plans, I mean."

"I'm not interested in the progress of your *plans,*" lied Hilda. "I rang to ask you for supper on Thursday."

"Thank you, Hilda. I'd be delighted. May I bring my fiancée with me if I have one by then?"

"Don't be silly, James."

And he had been silly. When he went over the top he lost his advantage. "Yes, I suppose that is somewhat optimistic. The usual time?"

"Of course, James. You have made me very unhappy. Goodbye."

"No need to be unhappy on my account, Hilda."

Hearing the growl of Hilda's replaced receiver James replaced his own and wandered over to the patio door to gaze out on the garden and encounter the intermittent dour gaze of his housekeeper's son Michael, hoeing one of the side beds. He tried to think about their plans for the garden, but his mind kept switching back to that terrible encounter with the first of the women he'd invited to dinner as a result of his notice in *The Times.* Despite her promising letter she had been dreary and common. (Angrily he stamped on Hilda's snobbish word, but it bounced back undamaged.) From the moment of meeting he had been assigned the role of listening post to which she would inevitably consign a husband. Dinner had seemed interminable as she expounded on her shallow, sentimental philosophy of life tight under its lacquer of ladylike gentility. She must have had advice when she wrote her letter; there had been no trace in that of the genteel. Although something in the features of the photograph had tried to give him pause.

It had been ten o'clock before he could interrupt the flow and bring the evening to an end. She had arrived by public transport, and reluctantly he had offered her a lift to the station. Beside him in the car she had been silent, and he was rehearsing his parting words, beginning to see his ordeal as over, when in a quiet suburban street she asked him to stop, so urgently he had thought she was carsick and had obeyed her.

And then she had launched herself upon him. Grimly, purposefully, with the terrible strength of need. He had had to get rough with her to free himself. . . .

James switched his gaze from the memory and back onto the garden. Michael was studying him covertly from his stooping position on the edge of the lawn, but as James caught his eye and smiled the man looked quickly down at the ground he was working on.

A funny old stick, Michael. Well, not old, of course. Probably only about forty. And really quite a good figure of a man if one thought about it, with a well-shaped head too and fine features behind the stubble for which no designer ideas were responsible. Not talking unless encouraged, but he'd said enough over the years to show that he'd educated himself with reading, and James had got into the habit of offering him the odd book. Dickens, Thackeray, Herman Melville . . . He always told people there was really nothing wrong with Michael, nothing to which you could give a name, he was just withdrawn. That was his mother's word for her son, and it would probably have been James's too without her prompting. Mrs. Moxon had told him Michael had always been that way, and blamed it on the lack of a father, Mr. Moxon having disappeared with another woman while his wife was confined. James sometimes wondered how much of Mrs. Moxon's intense solicitude came from a natural maternal wish to protect a vulnerable offspring, and how much from her immovable sense of personal responsibility for Michael's not having had the benefit of a father. It seemed to James that Mr. Moxon had been a good riddance, but Mrs. Moxon was unwavering in her belief that he was a loss and that the guilt for his disappearance was hers.

"Husbands don't go off, Mr. Marshall, if there's enough to keep them at home."

"Forgive me, Mrs. Moxon, but that's ridiculous. Some men just shouldn't get married at all; they can't take the responsibility, or be loyal, however wonderful their wives. And the way you look after me it's obvious you were wonderful."

"I'm sorry, Mr. Marshall, I don't want to argue with you, but John Moxon went off because I let him go."

The dialogue, subject to minor variations, was recurrent. Once James had asked her if there would ever come a time when her devotion of her life to Michael would earn her her own forgiveness.

"There'll never be enough that I can do for that boy, Mr. Marshall."

He presumed it to be the answer no.

Michael was looking at him again, from the other side of the lawn. Looking away. But when James went out to him he'd be straight-eyed and civil. . . .

Standing eventually in the road by the open car door, he'd told the dishevelled fury in the passenger seat that he'd take her wherever she wanted to go. But she'd got out of the car with a malevolent glare and started walking away from it as fast as her thin high heels would let her. He'd driven alongside, begging her to get back in and let him carry on to the station, but she'd ignored him. Then threatened to call a policeman. It was at this grotesque point that a taxi had cruised by and she had hailed it. He'd never forget the mixture of horror and relief with which he'd watched it dwindling from his car mirror.

And he was going to do it again. Once in London, then twice on home ground.

James turned from the window and began to pace about the room. He'd make it clear at the outset of both the Linton encounters that he'd be saying goodnight at the end of dinner. And he certainly wouldn't be issuing an invitation to his house the first time of meeting. If it was the right thing there would be plenty of time, and if it wasn't he wouldn't want them in his house anyway. . . .

"I'm off now, Mr. Marshall. Forgive me, I didn't mean to startle you."

He had jumped visibly. "It's all right, Mrs. Moxon. I was miles away."

"Watching Michael?" She came to the window, where he had ended his pacing.

"I started off watching Michael." She was a woman of such correctness and self-control, the fact of her presence at his side was somehow moving. "Then I was just staring into space, thinking. Mrs. Moxon . . ."

All at once he knew she was aware of his unease. "What is it, Mr. Marshall?"

"Mrs. Moxon, I've advertised for a wife." Only seconds ago he had not so much as considered telling her. "Should I have done such a thing?" He was crazy; it was Angela she had loved.

"You were so happy married, Mr. Marshall, I should say it was a very sensible idea." She wasn't even surprised. "And in your case a safe one. Meaning you've such a standard to keep up you won't settle for second best. Well, everyone after Mrs. Marshall has to be second best in a sense, if you'll excuse me for saying so. But you'll know that yourself."

"Of course." Her understanding warmed him. "It's because I was so happy with Angela that now I'm—"

"That's clear as day, Mr. Marshall. If you'll forgive me, though— did you say advertise? In the papers?" Apologetically he nodded. "There are agencies for it, you'd have been better with one of them. I mean to say, they find out the sort of person to suit you. Advertising in the papers . . ." To Mrs. Moxon "the papers," from *The Times* to *The News of the World,* were the source of every modern decadence.

"I expect you're right, Mrs. Moxon. I've seen one and she was awful. I'm seeing another in London next week"—he gestured vaguely towards his open desk and its litter—"then two more here after that. But I shan't ask them to the house the first time."

"That's wise, Mr. Marshall, if you'll excuse me for passing an opinion. If the lady's right there'll be plenty of time."

"Just what I thought, Mrs. Moxon."

"There is one other thing." Mrs. Moxon stirred on her small, trim feet, put up a hand to push a strand of colourless hair behind her ear.

"Yes, Mrs. Moxon?"

"I know I've no right to say what I'm going to say, and I'll be glad to accept it if you tell me I'm out of order. But—well, I wouldn't say nothing to your sister if I was you. Not until you've settled on a lady. Which I'm sure you will do eventual-like. And when you have . . . Well, I think it would be best if you told Mrs. Passy she'd come into the shop, say, or that you'd met at one of those dinner parties you're always trying not to go to."

"Mrs. Moxon, you're wonderful, you really are. I'd given myself that very piece of advice, and then when I had Hilda and Cyril to dinner the other night, Harry Venables came in and while I was making the coffee he went and told 'em. I couldn't blame him, he couldn't have known you and he were the only people I was going to let into my secret"—the corners of her eyes creased as they looked at one another—"but my sister was very upset. She telephoned just now and told me off again. It hasn't helped."

"You didn't ought to let Mrs. Passy worry you, Mr. Marshall, though it's a pity you didn't register with an agency. You do that, and keep your spirits up. And excuse me for talking out of turn."

"I'm very glad to have your views, Mrs. Moxon, believe me." He meant it, his spirits were already restored. And despite the excellent advice he was all at once optimistic again about his *Times* enterprise.

"It'll be all right, Mr. Marshall, you'll see. There's Michael, now. . . ." James in his turn was perceptive enough to realize it had been because of Michael that she had first come to stand beside him. "I worry about him, Mr. Marshall. More as time goes on. I used to think that when he was a man there'd be less worry, but it hasn't been like that. If I could just find someone for him, to look after him when I'm gone. He'd be all right with a good girl, he'd be honest and faithful. There's nothing wrong with him, Mr. Marshall, it's just that he's caught up inside himself, like, and off his own bat he'll never go halfway towards courting a woman. He's taught himself ever such a lot, if you heard him with me of an evening sometimes you'd be ever so surprised. He goes regular to the library and remembers what he reads, and he's ever so grateful for those books you give him. If he could just get confident and relaxed with a young woman like he is with me . . . I can do most things for him, Mr. Marshall, but I can't find him a wife."

"I don't know, Mrs. Moxon," said James carefully, after a few moments in which they both watched Michael covertly watching them as he continued his reflex work along the borders. "What you've just been saying to me . . . If you really feel Michael would be happier married, couldn't you go to one of these agencies yourself and tell them about him? They must have shy, withdrawn girls on their books."

"I've thought of it, Mr. Marshall. For him and for you. If you'll excuse me." The corners of her mouth twitched, briefly dislodging the habitual look of anxiety which accompanied her habitual concern for her son. "It's fine for you, as I've said, if you'll forgive me offering an opinion. But for Michael . . . Well, perhaps I will one of these days. I reckon it'll be the only way. But there's time enough yet, I've plenty of life left in me."

"Of course you have, Mrs. Moxon." James spoke absently, absorbed in his sudden recall of how three years ago the worst thing in life had seemed to him to be its continuance. He'd been almost shocked, the first time he had found himself looking forward to something, as if it was a betrayal of Angela. And now he was planning the ultimate betrayal. . . . He pulled himself back. "Don't miss your bus."

"I'm in plenty of time, but thank you, Mr. Marshall. And good luck, if you'll excuse me. I've left Michael's tea."

As he heard the click of the front latch James opened the door to the garden and strolled down to Michael.

"Looks good," he observed, after a few moments in which his gardener made no concession to his presence.

"Not too bad, I reckon." Michael straightened up, turning his gloomy gaze onto his employer. "This is a good spot, it's worth sweating at."

"Which you do, Michael. As if it was the only garden in the world. Still reading?"

"I've usually got a book on the go."

"That's good. I won't hold you up now." The man was beginning to fidget. Anyway, it was time he got back to the shop. "Your mother's put your tea out. Lock the back door when you're ready to leave, and go out the front way."

"Very good, Mr. Marshall."

Turning at the open patio door, James saw that in the time it had taken him to walk slowly back to the house Michael had transformed a weed-green slope to rich brown and was still furiously digging.

CHAPTER SEVEN

When she was ready Eve studied herself in her long mirror, regretting that she'd fallen out with the woman across the way. She'd like to have been able to ask her in and be told how lovely she looked, even if the woman didn't mean it. Have a single booster gin and tonic in company rather than the double she'd just finished on her own. Suddenly she felt deprived, ashamed even, at not having a woman friend she could have asked to be with her at this crucial moment.

She'd had them in the past, of course, encountered in her various jobs. But she'd always considered herself a man's woman and eventually, after she'd broken several dates for something more exciting, or met their boyfriends, they hadn't wanted to know. She never meant to take their boyfriends away from them, but somehow it tended to happen.

None of those women, though, had been real friends. The only real friend she had was Brenda.

Eve stared at her glamorous image in astonishment. Brenda! Brenda whose calm could be such an irritant, who she so often felt glad was looking increasingly pinched and middle-aged. But, yes, Brenda was more than an office colleague, Brenda was her friend. If only that slim, dark figure was behind her now in the glass, if only she was listening to Brenda's quiet, very slightly amused voice telling her the truth about her appearance!

But Brenda wasn't there. And neither was anybody else.

The voluptuous figure in front of her was no longer clear in the lamplight, it had begun to blur.

For God's sake don't start crying now, you stupid bitch, after spending all that time on your face and your eyes!

Out in the hall, to her relief and a pang of fear, the buzzer croaked. Dabbing cautiously at her lashes Eve leaned towards herself for the last time, nodding and smiling at the hazy impression of glowing feminine abundance, swirled into her shawl, made sure the envelope was in her bag. Then sped from the flat and down the stairs to her waiting taxi.

He was much too early, but somewhere in his subconscious he must have known he would want to stop. Sit in the car in a lay-by with the window down, telling himself he was still uncommitted, that he could still turn round and go home.

Uncommitted? He would be uncommitted at the end of the evening, too, for heaven's sake, he wasn't expected to propose to her that night. All he was doing was meeting an attractive woman for dinner. Giving himself an interesting night out.

Eve Harris. Eve the temptress. He hadn't got her photograph with him, but his memory reminded him how appropriately she was named. If she tempted him and he fell, and then she drew back like the other . . .

It would be all right this time, it wouldn't be like the other. And the other had been an accident, a piece of incredibly bad luck. He'd thought she was asking for it and he'd made the wrong move and then when she'd panicked . . . He must have found that nerve in the neck they called the death spot, everyone knew that it didn't take much pressure.

This time there wouldn't be any misunderstanding. This time they would both know what they wanted.

A lorry tore past, the waves of its wake thundering against the car. Engine oil hung on the fresh air, making him cough and then be aware of the contrasting beauty of the evening, mild and still and blue-skied. Even in the lay-by a spindly chestnut was putting out tiny, tight green fists. Perhaps after dinner they could go for a drive. To the Heath, where it would be quiet. And dark, it would be dark by then. Or they could even go . . .

He'd been lucky in the end, that other time, no one being about, no one seeing the car. He mustn't push that luck.

Not that he would, of course, he wasn't a fool. It was just that when certain feelings started up—feelings like anger and frustration—it was a struggle not to let them take over.

But tonight he'd be careful. If care was needed. He couldn't believe it would be.

Eve.

Leaning back in his seat he deliberately relaxed, preparing himself to command his entire small stock of self-control.

It wasn't just because of the beard that Eve knew the man at the corner table was James Marshall. Even before he got to his feet she'd noted the neat ears and well-shaped head of the photograph, the abundant brown hair. And now, when he was standing, there was the height. Six foot, the typed description had said. As she approached him he seemed even taller.

"Eve?" he asked softly, smiling, holding out his hand. His eyes were greeny-brown, deep set, something the photograph hadn't shown her. "I'm James Marshall."

Her hand was agreeably smooth and cool. She was a bit older than the photograph but as promising, experience and cynicism shining from her big blue eyes.

"Yes, I'm Eve."

"Sit down, Eve, won't you? I thought we might have our first drink together here at our table. Easier to relax. And more private." He hesitated, his smile fading and then turning into a grin. "I was going to say, easier for us both in a difficult situation. But suddenly it doesn't seem difficult after all."

"No," breathed Eve in sultry agreement, sinking into the chair he had pulled out. The remark had been slick, but the way he'd made it, and the way he'd grinned at her as he did, had saved it, even made her believe him. And it was true after all, her own nervousness had vanished.

"Well, Eve. What would you like to drink?"

She had gin and tonic like he did, and they sat smiling at each other while they drank. It was marvellous, and marvellously rare, not to feel she had to talk, not to find silence embarrassing. To start off like that promised well for the night . . . For a moment she'd forgotten she'd met this man in order to consider marrying him. There would have to be plenty of talk before they got round to *that*. But meanwhile she was actually enjoying herself. Ever since she'd answered the ad she'd imagined herself at this moment talking politely to an unglamorous middle-aged man, trying to bring her instincts into line with her intention of securing a husband. As it had turned out, it was easier to think of James Marshall as a desirable date than as a potential marriage partner. But marriage was what he was after, he had said so in his ad, then in his letter. Could it really be that her luck was turning at last?

"That was a good photograph, Eve. Professional, of course." She'd mentioned modelling in her CV, but she'd also mentioned working in an office. Modelling jobs no longer so easy to come by? Boyfriends thinner on the ground? She didn't seem the type to be looking for marriage, but she'd probably just realized time was marching on. The qualms which had accompanied him into the restaurant were subsiding, giving way to a growing sense of self-congratulation. Despite the photograph, and discreet indications in the CV of a varied life, he'd been afraid of finding himself facing a neurotic woman either hopelessly inhibited or else barely able to restrain her suppressed desires.

And he was facing Eve. He'd known it was his lucky night.

"The photographer knew all the tricks." Eve laughed in false self-deprecation, confident, for the moment at least, of her appeal. "Yours was a good photograph too, James."

He shrugged. "A man with a beard . . . A beard hides a weak chin, and doesn't show so much of a mouth, either."

"It doesn't hide the eyes. . . . Your mouth's all right, James. So are its contents, I gather."

"Sorry?" He couldn't think what she was talking about, but her own mouth was holding his eyes like a magnet.

" 'My beard is removable but my teeth are not.' "

She was quoting. "Ah, yes. I was rather pleased with that."

"It amused me. I've got my own teeth, too." But shouldn't be saying so, for God's sake, as if she was listing the good points of a cow at market. For the first time embarrassment swelled through her, and she remembered Brenda's warning not to go over the top. There was danger of it, Brenda had been right. "Not that it matters," she added quickly.

"Not that it matters." Lazily he smiled at her, smiling inside as well at the dismay which for an instant had darkened the beautiful eyes. But she was bound to be more strung up than he was. "Which reminds me that perhaps we ought to have a look at the menu."

"Yes. Lovely." She'd been lucky not to have destroyed the mood. She'd be more careful, now, not get too pleased with herself. If only it wasn't so important! It was probably a good idea to let herself think of this meeting as just another date, it would stop her getting anxious. And anyway it was hard to imagine James Marshall tackling the practical issues in the mood he'd engendered. He'd obviously decided they should get to know one another in the usual way, as if unaware of each other's long-term hopes.

"What's it to be then, Eve? Please choose exactly what you'd like, don't try to be economical."

"Thank you, James. I think I'd like whitebait to start. Then the duck." He mightn't really be generous, but meanness at this stage would have been a very bad sign.

"Wine?"

"I'll leave it to you."

"Fine." A sense of relief. He didn't need competition in that area, he considered himself a bit of a wine buff. And if he showed knowledge vis-à-vis the staff which she didn't possess it would probably impress her. He ordered a fillet steak, and when the wine waiter came over he went to town on the subject of burgundies.

Another waiter deposited their first course. "Must be fun running a book shop," observed Eve as he disappeared, wondering not for the first time if James Marshall's business was remunerative. She had already established that she'd be pleased to be seen with him. And no waiter would make the mistake of asking her what her father would like. On the other hand, there would be no danger of one asking James what they could get for his mother. . . .

"Cold?" he asked solicitously as she shivered.

"No, no. The goose on my grave."

"Oh, but not tonight!" He smiled at her.

"Not tonight, no. D'you enjoy the book shop, James?"

He knew his surge of anger was unreasonable. "Most of the time. Sometimes I hate it, but I'd be miserable if I didn't have it." He'd rehearsed that.

"I can understand." It must be a good living. Well, he had said it was. But people had different expectations. Her own, up to now, had been low. "New and secondhand books, you said. Do you have fabulously expensive first editions?"

"Not fabulously expensive." That was surely enough. "Eve, you're very beautiful."

"Thank you." But her pleasure was shot through with unease. On such a serious, long-term project he should be taking his time. She had thought she was treating the evening in her usual way, but underneath she wasn't, underneath it felt like life or death. On the other hand, she was glad he wasn't asking her about her cooking. Suddenly her mood was light again. "Pretty, perhaps."

"Beautiful. Whitebait all right?"

"Delicious. Tell me about Linton."

His smile came back slowly. "It's a pretty little place. Changes with the weather. At least from where I live. I can see the sea."

"How *wonderful.*" She loved the sea. When she saw it she always had a sense of arriving where she needed to be.

"Yesterday it was more green than blue." He'd stood beside it, looking to the horizon. "Sometimes it's grey like steel. It can look like the Mediterranean."

"D'you get a lot of tourists?"

Linton took them through the main course as well, interspersed with Eve's doctored recollections of her childhood home in the leafy London suburb, whose influence on her life she greatly exaggerated. And her first marriage, now, was a whirlwind romance which hadn't survived its early rapture.

"Don seemed so exciting when I was seventeen. Mummy and Daddy weren't very happy about it, but they came up trumps and gave us a lovely wedding." She had no difficulty. Increasingly over the years, the lovely wedding of her imagination had become more real to her than the short ceremony in Catford Register Office from which she and Don had gone straight to bed. "You had a good marriage, James."

"I did, Eve. Perhaps I'll be able to talk about it eventually."

"I'm sorry, I shouldn't have . . ." But in his CV he'd sounded unafraid of the sacred past. "I suppose it was easier on paper."

"That's it. Easier than talking. I'm sorry, I still find it difficult."

The waiter, with impeccable timing, was beside them. "Do have a lovely big pudding."

"I couldn't." She hoped she was reassured. "I'd just like a coffee."

"Two coffees, please."

With the coffee a slight restraint set in. The end of the evening was all at once in sight, needing to be got through to mutual satisfaction. In the contrived circumstances, neither of them could see so much as a step ahead.

If he says goodbye and I'll ring you, that'll be it. Eve spelled it out in her head, determined to preempt the worst by expecting it. And his smiles and his compliments had given her no real idea of her effect on him.

He looked surreptitiously at his watch. Time to call it a day. Not push his luck. "Look, Eve, we're having a good evening, I don't want to call it a day yet, and I hope you don't." She murmured, smiling. "How about driving out to Linton? It won't take more than an hour, an hour and a half, at this time of night and we can talk in the car." He put on his self-deprecating grin. "Unless of course you feel—"

"I'd love to drive to Linton, James." The daze engendered by such unaccustomed success helped her not to sound too eager.

"We can leave your car here and I can—"

"My car's in dock." Eve manufactured a rueful grimace. Time enough to tell him she'd decided to sell her nonexistent car. "I took a taxi."

"Then it's easy. When we get back I can take you straight home."

"But . . . That'll mean you'll be driving most of the night. You'll have to go all the way back to Linton again." Perhaps it was all a ploy to get her to have him stay with *her*. Under the table Eve crossed her fingers.

"You're thoughtful, Eve, but it's all right, I'm staying in London tonight. I'm seeing a London book dealer first thing in the morning and a friend's putting me up. He's given me his key." James took a Yale key out of his pocket. "Yes, I've still got it. So I can let myself in any time. How about it?"

She could still hardly believe her ears. "Well . . . that's all right then, James. Let's—let's go."

"Yes, let's go." He got up and went over to the bar to pay the bill, no messing about with it in front of her. He came back with her shawl. "Hope you'll be warm enough." His hands lingered briefly on her shoulders, provoking a sensation she was unable to define. Not quite the usual looking forward. But her anticipations were not those she was accustomed to after a successful dinner—the hands that had arranged her shawl tonight might be arranging it for the rest of her life. The prospect was so overwhelming it was affecting her normal responses. Which, anyway, she knew she ought for the moment to keep in check.

"Oh, I'll be warm enough, James."

She smiled at him over her shoulder, and he felt again the dual surge of anger and excitement. He should take her home. But he heard himself telling her there was a rug in the car.

They drove mostly in silence, and after a few minutes he put the radio on. She didn't mind, if they didn't talk she couldn't make a mess of things, and it was good just to relax to music and contemplate the miraculous fact that he'd asked her to stay with him long beyond the time he could have politely said goodbye. And not for the usual reason. A couple of times he put his hand lightly on hers, but didn't leave it there or move it anywhere else.

"There's a new road," he said, when they were an hour or so clear of London and speed limits. "I haven't used it yet in the dark. If we get lost don't think I've done it on purpose." His profile smiled.

"Of course I won't." She was more and more reassured.

The car surged on. James wouldn't lose his way. . . .

"There's the sea!"

She jumped, she had actually fallen asleep. "Is this Linton?"

"Almost."

He had pulled up. To their right there was nothingness, but to their left the world shimmered out of sight under the moon.

"Oh, James!"

"Beautiful, isn't it?" He felt enormously exhilarated. "Let's get out. Smell the ozone. I don't want to stop actually in Linton, my car's rather well known and my sister's staying with me and likes to mind my business. I want to take you in openly, in daylight." His eyes glittered at her. "The sea and the sand are just as good here. And the tide's out." Yes, it was his lucky night. "We could walk a little."

"I understand, James, of course." She supposed she did. She lowered her window. "It's a lovely night. Yes, I wouldn't mind a walk." She peered past him, across the road. "No street lights, just as well there's a moon. What's over there?"

"Sand dunes." The moonlight showed him her smile. Again he felt the dual surge of anger and excitement. He should turn round and go back to London.

But he got out of the car and went round to her door.

"All right? The sand shouldn't be too wet. . . . Heavens, I forgot you weren't dressed for it."

"This shawl's warmer than it looks and I can take my shoes off." But he was draping the rug round her shoulders.

"Steady now!" She had stumbled and he had caught her arm, was continuing to hold it as they walked down the rough slope which shone where the moonlight caught the drapes of seaweed. "You're still cold!"

"No, really." Her shiver had been her acknowledgment of her frustration, her awareness of potential release at her side. It seemed a long time since Rodney had gone, and anyway he had never been much good. James Marshall promised to be different.

She shivered again. She mustn't let her short-term needs destroy her future. She mustn't be so downright stupid. She'd had so much already, and if she restrained herself tonight she might have James Marshall for every night to come. And if she blew it, her self-contempt would make life even less worth living than it was already.

"Just a few minutes, then I suppose we ought to start back." She had to force the words out.

"Of course." Perhaps they should. Oh yes, they should. But he was leading her along the sands. "It's beautiful, though, isn't it? Look at the moon."

"Oh yes, James, it's beautiful." And so wonderfully romantic, the moon throwing them a golden path across the calm sea, the air like wine. At some point his hand had slid down her arm and was holding hers. Her heels were sinking into the sand and her feet were cold and damp but that was somewhere miles away. "Which way is Linton?"

"The way the car's facing. If we walked a few miles this way we could look back at it. But this bit's quite wild and lonely." He realized that was why he'd chosen it, why he was listening for human sounds, hoping he wouldn't hear them. "Eve . . . It's been a lovely evening."

"It has, James. Really. And some sea air was just what I needed after that marvellous dinner and the drive. But time to be getting back . . ."

Nevertheless she had turned to him, he thought he could feel her breasts against his noisy heart. "Of course. Yes." He made his last effort. "And I know we don't want to spoil—the future. But we've got on so well, haven't we? Haven't we, Eve?"

"Oh, yes, James!" Oh, it was all right. He had mentioned the future in a way which showed that after several hours in her company he saw her as part of it. And they would have to find out if they were physically compatible, too. No point in going on with things if they weren't.

She raised her face as his arms came round her. His first kiss, gently intimate, had her tottering, and she offered no resistance as he led her towards a tall outcrop of rock. "We're too old for the back of the car, wouldn't you say?"

"James . . ."

"Here, don't you think?" He took the rug from her shoulders and spread it at the foot of the rock, facing the sea. "Eve . . ."

Thoughts of her dress, shawl and shoes were fleeting. Anyway, the shoes must already be ruined. One came off as she dropped gracefully to the sand. "James . . ." He was on the rug too, leaning over her, helping her to lie down. The moonlight glittered on his wide, unwavering eyes, blurring and disappearing as she felt the furry softness of his beard. Gently, gently . . . Whatever she had permitted in the long, monotonous tunnel of her life, it had had to be gentle. A gentle progress towards the goal she so seldom denied. But roughness had always been her turn-off. James would be gentle.

Take it easy, he told himself. Eve. Eve the temptress. But she wasn't, she was as kind as she was lovely, drawing him to her, making him welcome. It was all right, he had known it would be; as soon as he'd seen that photograph he'd known he wanted the very heart of her.

Was going to have it.

"James!" He wasn't gentle, he was powerfully, roughly ahead of her, hurting her mouth, her breasts, putting all her desires to flight. "James!" Dear God, she couldn't live with this, not tonight, not any time! This was the sort of thing she never put up with. She'd thought he was different, but now . . . James Marshall! Well, you never knew. Thank goodness, thought Eve as she struggled, that she'd given in to her weakness, found out at an early stage that it wasn't going to work. Next time she'd be positively glad to see that fatherly, middle-aged gentleman.

"James! Please! Let me go!"

She was struggling more and more desperately, and his anger was back. Eve Harris was the biggest tease he'd met, worse even than that other one, letting him get so close to her and now trying to shut him out. Stabbing her fingers at his eyes, trying to raise her knees against him . . .

"Bitch! Bitch!" For a moment he heard his voice above hers, but as his anger and frustration grew it was her voice that dominated, wailing out hideously in that great deserted space. He'd have to stop it.

She bit his hand when he put it across her mouth and, cursing, he lowered it to her neck, bringing the other one up in an effort to control her. She could only gurgle now, but her arms and legs were still an irritant, pinching and bruising him and messing up his suit.

"Bitch!" The only way he could control those threshing limbs was from the neck, the master place. The master spot. He was so angry he was even feeling for it although he didn't know where it was. Red-headed bitch, serve her right for smiling at him, leading him on, bringing him here, lying down on his rug, and then denying him. . . .

The arms and legs were still now, and when he let go of the neck the head fell to one side. The sands were as quiet as when they'd climbed down to them. He and Eve. His anger had gone, leaving him cold and trembling and horribly afraid.

"Eve! For God's sake get up! I'll take you home." He caught at the anger as it growled away from him, but it eluded him, and he shivered and moaned. She wouldn't get up. She couldn't. He had done it again.

He didn't know how long he sat there, staring up at the moon. When he looked at his watch it was half past midnight, and although he hadn't been able to recapture his anger he was now comfortingly sorry for himself. She shouldn't have behaved like that, she'd as good as committed suicide.

His mind was back under his control. Fingerprints didn't show on skin and anyway, if he was lucky the police wouldn't be looking for them. The moonlight showed him her handbag on the edge of the rug. After tying his handkerchief round his hand he opened the bag and took out the envelope. It was difficult to get hold of the contents with one hobbled hand, but he managed it by holding the envelope between his knees. When he saw what he had taken out he laughed his satisfaction aloud—there was no one to hear him.

CHAPTER EIGHT

Sally slid into Linton without having to drive through any industrial or suburban sprawl. One moment she saw the sea across fields, the next she had descended a hill between intermittent cottages and was beside a high blue-green tide faced by bungalows in protective gardens which eventually gave way to a few blocks of Victorian boarding houses, culminating in the elegant white facade of the Grand Hotel.

Sally drew up on the sea side and let down her window, instantly aware of tangy marine air. Before her the bay curved on in a mirror image of the buildings she had just passed: red brick and cream stuccoed boarding houses, then the low spaced bungalows. The Grand Hotel was the keystone of an arch, the whole of it sparkling in the brilliant, cool spring sunshine.

For a moment she was entirely, mindlessly happy, but as she wondered on which side of Linton James Marshall lived the uneasiness crowded back and she started the engine again and followed the discreet notice down the side of the Grand.

Behind the hotel there was plenty of room for her car. Retrieving her case from the boot, crossing to the rear door, Sally found herself already alert for tall, bearded men.

"Mrs. Graham? Ah, yes." The girl in Reception smiled in a friendly way as she asked Sally to register, but she didn't know Sally's shameful secret.

Not shameful, Sally crossly corrected herself, merely a secret. Her own business. That was why she hadn't told anyone but Gill, not even her two good friends Helen and Laura, one of them still with a beloved husband, the other never having had or wanted one.

Gill had approved, had paused for a mere moment at the thought of her father.

"Gill, it's absurd, but in a way it's because Daddy and I were so happy."

"I know, Mummy, I understand."

"Your key, Mrs. Graham. Two-four-seven on the second floor."

The room was a wedge-shape, on a corner half overlooking the sea. One of the most dismal things since Tom died had been single rooms in hotels, but this one was so unusual, its enormous window turning the sky into extra private space, Sally didn't suffer the usual bleak reaction. Briefly happy again, she walked to the magnet of the view and pushed up one of the old sash panes. Two floors up she could still smell the sea, and when she leaned out she could see the curve of the bay to each side of her, two arms embracing that moving, multicoloured expanse of water, its white edge separated from the low wall by a pale sliver of sand. Men, women, children and dogs were passing each other slowly and with pauses engineered mostly by the dogs. Despite the risk of a premature encounter with a tall, bearded man she wanted to go out and become part of the everyday world of the promenade.

Turning to a mirror Sally tidied her hair, then almost ran out of the room on the realization that she had been looking at herself as James Marshall might see her.

It was as agreeable by the sea as she had imagined. The people she passed looked as though they lived in Linton, and her conversations with dogs engendered smiles and a few words with their owners. Towards the far end of the bay she dropped onto a seat beside the large female owner of a game-faced mongrel with pricked ears, and found herself being told about the difference between summer and winter Linton.

"It's sort of halfway at the moment, like it always is in April. And October. We like it, don't we, Benjy? Not deserted like the winter, but not so crowded as it is in summer. It's a nice place, really."

"Yes, I can see." She could. Even while disapproving of the way she was wondering whether she would be happy to live there. Time enough for that when she'd met James Marshall and got over the innumerable hurdles which merely to think about made her feel weary.

Only all at once she wasn't. All at once this small seaside town was under her skin and she was feeling cheerful and adventurous instead of apprehensive and ashamed. Seeing her pleasure in Linton as one hurdle already surmounted. If she and James Marshall were going to hit it off it was important to approve the place where she would have to live. And if she found she didn't want to meet him a second time that wouldn't spoil the three days in this charming place which lay before her. Meanwhile, the very fact of not knowing how the evening would turn out was making her feel alive.

For the first time in three years. *Oh, Tom!*

"You on holiday?" The large woman at her side turned with difficulty to look at her.

"Yes. I chose Linton with—with a pin on a map. I think I've been lucky."

"Well, I hope you enjoy yourself. As I said, it's a nice place. Have to go now, shopping won't take care of itself. Come along, Benjy."

Slow woman, and quick dog solicitously adapting its pace, moved gradually away. Sally sat on for a while contentedly watching the sea, and when she got up and turned her back on it she saw there was no jarring rise behind the buildings which lined the bay.

A nice place.

Back in her room she made tea and took it to the window, watching small boats and trying to hang on to her new sense of relaxation. Some places, like some people, took a long time to get to know or remained resistant, but Linton was friendly and extrovert, ready to share its charms. However James Marshall turned out to be, she didn't think he was like the town where he lived; he had presented himself on paper as reticent, shy, slow to reveal his treasures. Like herself.

But what treasures did she have to reveal?

It was a bit like an exam, pursued Sally as she poured a second cup, where you'd done your homework or you hadn't. You couldn't add to your capacities on the way into the examination room. Either life had formed her and James Marshall to be agreeable to each other, or it hadn't. Now for heaven's sake let her leave it there!

Smiling, Sally stood up and put her head out of the window. The sun was still shining, but its rays were more sharply angled along the promenade, and the colours of land and sea were muting. Gulls were tossing and crying, a mournful yet welcome sound making her feel nostalgic for something which until the moment of hearing it she was unaware of having lost. The air tapped her cheek, reminding her it was early April, and she took a stout handle in either hand and pulled the window down.

"Not tonight, darling. I know I'm walking, but it's not just a walk. I shan't be late. Be a good girl and take care of the house."

James patted Heidi, and with large-eyed reproach she slumped down into an untidy circle in the centre of the sitting-room floor. He looked yet again at the clock. A quarter to seven, he'd have to start, he couldn't put it off any longer.

He wasn't going to the dentist, for heaven's sake, he told himself angrily as he closed the gate. Nor was he lowering a drawbridge for an enemy to creep in. No one would come to the White House unless he invited them. It must be the horror of that other encounter which was making him so reluctant. And so ridiculously illogical. What had happened between him and that woman had nothing to do with Sally Graham.

It was a glorious evening. He'd been too busy to get home for lunch, and this was the first time he had been able to savour the air of the glorious day every other one of his customers had assured him he was missing. Linton looked pretty, its surfaces red-gold under the low departing sun. Why hadn't he left things as they were, been grateful for health and strength and friends and his awareness still of Angela? What he had done had made him unaware of her now except as a fact, his first wife who had died.

Sally Graham. The impact of her photograph had been pleasing, and he had liked the tone of her letter. She had made the best impression on him of the four possible responses to his ad. Surely he would at least find her an agreeable dinner date?

What, though, would she think of him?

The sudden self-doubt, the switch in thought from his own reactions to the reactions of the woman awaiting him, seemed to ease and steady him; a sense of defensive manhood was easier to carry than fear for his future. Squaring his shoulders, James glanced at himself in a plate-glass window, then increased his snail's pace towards the Grand Hotel.

Perhaps it was the improvement in her mood, but her hair and face and clothes all seemed for once to do what she wanted, and as she stood at a minute to seven in front of the glass Sally knew she looked as attractive as she ever could look. Well, that was like the choice of pen to take into the exam, the only part of things over which, at this stage, she had control.

At least, thank goodness, there was no more time for panic philosophy.

She walked past the lift and down the two wide, curved staircases at a regular, steadying pace, regretting her vulnerability as she rounded the final turn. Either she would be watched in the long, last part of her descent, or he wouldn't be there and it would be much more noticeable to come to an indecisive halt at the foot of a grand staircase than after sidling out of a lift. . . .

"Sally! How very nice to see you!"

He was there, coming forward with his hand out as she left the last stair, acting for the benefit of the watching staff as if they were old friends, thinking of how she must be feeling, saving her embarrassment. And having no doubt who she was. He had studied her photograph and was telling her it was a true likeness. Whether she would have recognized him from his photograph she didn't know.

"James! Lovely to see you!"

Her handshake was cool and firm, she smiled with her eyes. It was astonishing the way she fulfilled the promise of her photograph. Photographs could capture a moment so rare—a moment of refinement, say, in a coarse face—that the reality turned out almost unrecognizable. But Sally Graham's photograph had shown her as she was. Not just the elfin face and naturally fair hair. The look, too, of shy integrity just managing to suppress a smile.

But he couldn't really have seen all that in her photograph; he mustn't go overboard on the strength of an appearance, a handclasp, a smile. He must be careful. Not risk getting himself into trouble again.

"Shall we go to the bar and have drinks while we order?"

"Lovely." She'd said "lovely" already, but James Marshall had proved himself sensitive enough to realize she was facing an ordeal. As he was, too, although it didn't show in the steady eyes which smiled as well as the mouth. She would like to have seen more of the mouth, but the beard was luxuriant. *My beard is removable but my teeth are not.* Perhaps she could persuade him . . . Shocked, Sally blocked off that line of thought as she perched on the bar stool. But it had shown her there was a chance of her at least enjoying the evening.

"What would you like to drink, Sally?"

"Dry sherry?"

"Of course."

He ordered the same for himself, handed her the menu, made a few tentative suggestions on the strength of his knowledge of the Grand Hotel cuisine. Choosing was an agreeable process, and when their decisions were made he asked her if she was comfortable in the hotel.

"Oh, yes. My room's on the corner and my window looks over the sea." There would be inevitable embarrassments, such as thoughts engendered by the subject of bedrooms, and she hastened on. "Linton's a very pretty place."

"It is, isn't it? I'm happy living here. I couldn't imagine, now, being away from the sea." He hadn't meant to imply that if anything developed between them he would refuse to move inland, although that might be the truth. This first evening, at least, the way would be strewn with pitfalls. He hurried away from this one. "But one never knows what will happen. I mean . . ." He had immediately fallen into another. Ruefully he screwed up his face and was delighted but not surprised when she smiled and then laughed.

"I know. It's bound to be a bit difficult, isn't it? I was so grateful the way you greeted me as if we were friends. I mean . . ."

"I felt we were." He didn't think he had, but he did now. Already the meeting at the foot of the stairs seemed a long way in the past. "But apart from that, I thought it would be easier so far as the surrounding eagle-eyed personnel were concerned. Perhaps even more for me than for you." She had taken this piece of honesty with a smile, too. "I'm not unknown in this small town, and I prefer to keep my private life to myself."

"Of course, yes." How self-absorbed she had been, not appreciating that! "I should have realized, but I was thinking about myself." It was marvellous to know she could say that.

"Of course you were."

"How's your dog?" Heavens, he might think she was already angling for an invitation to his house! Again she hurried on. "Did you bring her and leave her in the car? Dogs would rather sit in the car for hours than be left at home, wouldn't they? That's the difficulty with cats, I hate leaving mine, even for an evening, but he wouldn't thank me for taking him with me." That was *enough!* She mustn't let nervousness make her talk too much. And she didn't have the excuse of nervousness—she felt relaxed, even happy.

"I walked here tonight, so Heidi had to stay at home. What have you done with your cat tonight?"

Of course, he believed she had abandoned Blackie for only one night. "I've left him at home. He has the cat flap and a neighbour devoted to him, so I know he'll be all right. I still worry though, of course."

"Of course." It couldn't be as marvellous as it seemed, it simply couldn't. Already he could take her in his arms, but no more eagerly than he already longed to discover the whole cast of her mind. "You can take a dog about with you, and more and more hotels seem to be prepared to take them."

"I like dogs too—I like all animals—well, you know." Her smile was mischievous; she saw humour in their contrived courtship, which delighted him. "It's just that I'm first and foremost a cat person."

"I'd have guessed it. You have some of their qualities." It was a compliment.

"Thank you!"

"More sherry?"

"No."

"Wine, though?"

"Please. Your choice."

She would not, he already knew, be as amenable on all issues. She would tell him what she thought, what she felt, what she believed, treating them both first and foremost as people. But he couldn't know all this, he'd been talking to her casually for no more than a quarter of an hour. "Did you bring any paintings, Sally?"

"Paintings? Oh! No, I didn't." For a moment she hadn't understood him, but he was telling her he would like to see her work, realizing that he couldn't get to know her properly without seeing it. Something Geoffrey hadn't realized in six months.

"You should have. I shan't let you go home in the morning until I've dragged you round Better Books."

He stopped abruptly, colour flooding what she could see of his face. He had told her, within minutes of their meeting, that he wanted to see her again! His blush told her he knew it, too, and was surprised by his precipitation. She was as sure as she could be of anything that he had taken himself unawares, hadn't announced a plan for tomorrow morning in order to ensure her compliance for tonight.

"You won't need to drag me, I'd love to see your shop."

"Would you, Sally? Well, you shall." He knew he had blushed, in dismay as well as embarrassment. He might have spoiled things with the hastiness that had overtaken him. But her eyes were if anything brighter and more direct upon him, her smile more radiant. He had done no harm, and he had learned she would like to see him again.

There was so much to talk about they were the last people left in the dining room. Even then James didn't want to go, but he wanted her to know he intended saying goodnight at the table.

"What time shall I come in the morning?" he asked when he had paid the bill.

"At whatever time it's easiest for you to leave the shop." Anxiety continued to ebb away. After only a few minutes she'd felt his interest wasn't in the short term, and now she was sure.

"But it's you who is leaving. What's the latest you can stay, Sally?"

She hardly hesitated. "I'm on holiday. I've booked in here for another four nights. Not taking for granted it would be anything to do with you, James."

The mischief was there again, lightly veiling uncertainty. "I'm glad you decided to tell me. Have you decided what you want to do with your holiday?"

"I just thought I'd drive and walk, in and out of Linton. Be glad I'm not in school."

"I have two highly reliable assistants. May I take the day off tomorrow and be your guide? After you've seen the shop, of course."

He was almost confident of her reply, but he thought he had never more anxiously awaited an answer.

"Of course."

He got to his feet. "That's wonderful. If I come at ten? That will give you a chance to wake when you're ready and take your time over breakfast. Two essentials of a holiday."

"Ten will be fine."

"For me too." The incredulous joy running through him was unlike any sensation he could remember. It threatened to send a balloon through the top of his head which would lift him off the ground, and he forced himself to call on his native caution to hold him down. And anyway, feet on the ground made the best foundation.

"Walking up the stairs is different from walking down. You'll take the lift?"

He left her at the lift doors, holding her hand a fraction longer than was necessary. For Sally it was a strange dual sensation, longing for him to do more and being glad he didn't. Upstairs she tore to her window, wondering if she would see him on the promenade, but it was deserted save for an old man and a dog motionless side by side at the sea wall. She didn't even know in which direction he had set out for home. She knew, though, that tomorrow—or the day after—she would find out.

CHAPTER NINE

"Still no word from Eve, Brenda?"

"Brenda?"

Miss Griswold, standing a little behind Mr. Smith, appeared to have assumed the role of chorus. Normal service had to be seriously disrupted to merit a joint visit by Mr. Smith and Miss Griswold to Brenda and Eve's office.

"I'm afraid not, Mr. Smith." Even through her anxiety Brenda was aware of the small pleasure of being able to ignore Miss Griswold. "I tried telephoning her several times last night, as well as the night before, but there was no reply. I thought of going to see her, but she lives on the other side of London and if she was at home she'd answer the telephone."

Wouldn't she?

"One would imagine so, Brenda."

"One would imagine so," murmured Miss Griswold.

Mr. Smith looked testily over his shoulder. "Although if it was out of order—"

"I asked the engineer to check. He said it was ringing out all right."

"And even if it wasn't," pursued Mr. Smith, "that would scarcely prevent her from coming to work."

"It would perhaps prevent her from telling us why she couldn't, Mr. Smith. If she's ill . . ." Brenda had to make a small effort to hide the fresh wave of anxiety. "Look, I'll call on her tonight, I'll go straight from work."

"I'd appreciate it, Brenda."

". . . appreciate it." Miss Griswold backed away slightly under Mr. Smith's fierce eye.

"I should have gone last night."

"It really is most inconsiderate of her." Mr. Smith's annoyance could no longer be contained. "Most inconsiderate!"

"She tends to be late," stated Miss Griswold on an access of courage. "But I have never known her to take the day off—two days!—without telephoning with some excuse."

"Genuine or—er—otherwise," added Mr. Smith, wresting back the initiative. It was like a music hall turn, and Brenda had to bite her lip to keep from smiling. Not that, really, she felt like it. "I fancy sometimes Eve's excuses have been a little—suspect, but she has always let us know when she would be absent from the office."

Yes, Eve had. In her own way she had been conscientious, thought Brenda, trying yet again to stifle a surge of apprehension. And as a temp, strictly she had no need to offer any excuse at all for not coming in, she wasn't paid for her absences. But she had wanted to hold on to her job.

"When she left on Tuesday night, Brenda . . ." Mr. Smith clearly felt distaste for what he was being constrained to ask her. "Was she—did she seem—just as usual?"

"Oh, yes, Mr. Smith. In fact—she was rather cheerful."

On her way to meet James Marshall.

"I noticed it!" announced Miss Griswold, her eyes shining at her achievement of having secured all of Mr. Smith's attention. "I met her at the top of the stairs as she was leaving. She almost knocked me down. She apologized, of course, but there was some—some sort of excitement in her manner of which I could scarcely be unaware. You didn't notice it, Mr. Smith?"

Miss Griswold smiled her triumph, seeming to stretch upwards in demonstration of her one unarguable advantage over her senior —that of height. Mr. Smith was a man of small, rotund physique; Miss Griswold was tall and angular. As a pair they were comically illmatched, but Brenda had still not decided whether Miss Griswold aspired to overtake her widowed boss in the office hierarchy, or was setting her cap for him. Both ambitions, anyway, were equally over-pitched.

"I didn't notice it, Miss Griswold, because on Tuesday I saw Eve Harris only in the morning. If you recall, it was you who brought me the letters she had typed for signature. So, Brenda, we have no

—er—clue in Eve's behaviour on Tuesday? She said nothing—untoward—to you?"

"Nothing, Mr. Smith."

Nothing untoward in the context of what Eve had been saying ever since she'd answered James Marshall's ad in *The Times*. Perhaps she'd feel she had to tell Mr. Smith something more eventually, but not yet. Not until she'd given Eve a longer grace. And been to her flat. Which was to be loyal to Eve, wasn't it? If only she didn't keep getting these surges of anxiety. . . .

"Very well, Brenda. There is nothing for it but to implement the contingency operation Miss Griswold and I have been discussing." Miss Griswold's look of triumph told Brenda the operation was something she was unlikely to welcome. "Miss Griswold has been in touch this morning with the secretarial agency which sent Eve to us and has reported her non-appearance—"

"Oh, Mr. Smith!"

"I'm sorry, Brenda, I appreciate that you feel a certain loyalty towards Eve, but we are running a business. She has not had the grace to inform her agency, either, of her decision not to come to work. Fortunately the agency is able to supply us this afternoon with another young lady."

"But Eve can come back when she—when she comes back?" Even Brenda was for a moment at a verbal loss.

"If she has any sort of a convincing explanation. You must appreciate, Brenda, that otherwise I would be condoning any further whim she might have to take time off."

"Yes, of course, Mr. Smith." But her anxiety was growing more and more unmanageable. "As you've got another girl coming in this afternoon, might I take an extended lunch hour and go over to Eve's flat then? If there's no reply I just might find out something from a neighbour. I'll eat a sandwich on the tube."

"I think you might very well do that, Brenda. Visit Eve's flat, I mean. So far as the sandwich is concerned, I think you might venture to eat that in a sandwich bar; I am not a slave driver." Something in his manner told Brenda Mr. Smith was relieved at her offer, but he had still, of course, to present his compliance with it as a favour. "Perhaps you would like to go and telephone the agency, Miss Griswold. Ask for the new girl to arrive promptly at two. So far as your visit to Eve's flat is concerned, Brenda, I suggest you leave early—say twelve o'clock—and aim to be back here at your usual time so that you can show the new lady the ropes. Does that strike you as reasonable?"

Sometimes, for no discernible reason, Mr. Smith lurched into facetiousness.

"Absolutely, Mr. Smith. I'll get back to work on this document now, so that I have it ready for you before I go."

But following the immediate evacuation of her office, Mr. Smith urging the more reluctant Miss Griswold in front of him, Brenda didn't resume typing, she sat staring across her machine at Eve's empty chair as her thoughts churned.

She and Eve were only acquaintances; there had to be someone who knew her properly, knew why she hadn't come to work. Unless . . . But even if there was someone, that didn't explain Eve's absence the day after her date with James Marshall, and the day after that, and no telephone call.

Perhaps they'd got on so well she'd gone off with him then and there. It was the sort of thing Eve might do. She didn't want to queer Eve's pitch if that had happened—she wouldn't want anyone to queer hers in similar circumstances. (Brenda thought of Barry and winced.) And she didn't want to get mixed up in something which wasn't anything to do with her yet just might land her in a whole lot of trouble. . . .

Eve's old office cardigan hung askew on the back of her chair, and the forlorn look of it, reflecting Brenda's reluctant new image of its owner, smote suddenly through her cautious, tiptoeing thoughts, putting them contemptuously to flight. Poor Eve. Poor, warm, generous, hopeless Eve! She and Eve were more than acquaintances, they were friends. Eve might envy her—Brenda knew she did—but she was fond of her; she'd even said, once, that Brenda was her only friend, and then she'd tried to take it back in case Brenda found it an intrusion on her privacy. But Brenda had been pleased by this evidence of Eve's affection. So why hadn't she let Eve know?

Because she was a cold fish, that was why. But this wasn't the time for worrying about herself, it was the time for finishing Mr.

Smith's document so that she could get herself to Eve's flat and see if she was in need of help.

Stifling a fresh wave of uneasiness at her choice of phrase, Brenda began accurately and speedily to type, and at half-past eleven was putting the completed document on Mr. Smith's desk.

"I thought if there was nothing else at the moment, Mr. Smith, I might be on my way. . . ." There was a sort of masochistic pleasure in showing humility to this pompous little man whom in reality she despised. It was part of the punishment she deserved for having misled Barry all those years, for being a monster.

"Of course, Brenda." Mr. Smith's pores were oozing generosity as well as the perspiration which gleamed as always on his rosy temples. "Off you go."

From Baker Street she was able to go straight through on the Bakerloo Line to Kilburn Park. She had never visited Eve and had only a printed guide to lead her through increasingly down-at-heel streets to the big gloomy house, lone Victorian survivor marooned in an untended garden among blocks of postwar flats with blue and yellow plastic balconies. There was a cracked, weedy path up to the locked and still stout front door set in the exact centre of the peeling stucco facade.

Brenda looked down the numbers beside the vertical row of bells. Number six, that was Eve, although the slot beside the number was empty. Brenda rang the bell several times, but there was no response. There was none from number five, but on her second attempt at number seven there came a crackling sound and then a woman's tired voice.

"Yes? What is it?"

"Forgive me for disturbing you. I'm trying to contact Eve Harris."

"I don't know anything about Eve Harris." A sudden edge? "Anyway, she's out all day at work."

"That's just it!" Brenda, as always, had to push herself to sound eager. "I'm from her office and she hasn't shown up for a couple of days. Or telephoned. That's why I've come round. I'm worried." Silence. "Are you still there?"

"Yes, I'm here. Look, you'd better come in. I've got a key of Eve's, as a matter of fact. She gave it me when she first moved in and although we've not seen each other in months I never got around to giving it her back. Press the door when you hear the buzzer. Second floor."

The hall was narrow, its darkness shot through with red and green from the original glass in the front door. Brenda paused for a moment at the top of the second steep flight, her breathlessness exaggerated by her sudden panic. The door to the front of the house bore a tottering figure seven and was opposite the door numbered six.

Brenda might have knocked there first, but number seven was opening and a woman was appearing, standing watching her as she let go of the bannister rail and crossed the landing.

"Forgive me for bothering you, I'm Brenda Newbury from Mace and Edwards, where Eve works. Here . . ." She'd shoved a piece of letterhead into her bag last thing before leaving the office, and she held it out with her driving license.

"That's all right." Languidly the woman waved them away. She was wearing a pale pink satin dressing gown with food stains on the lapels. Her hair was untidy, and behind her Brenda caught a glimpse of an unmade bed through another open door.

"I'm sorry, are you ill?"

"I don't really know." The woman gave a sudden loud laugh.

There was no possible response. "Look, if you're satisfied I'm all right, I'll be grateful if you feel able to give me the key and I'll just go in and see if there's anything . . ." *Oh, Eve, don't be there!* "If Eve's there she's obviously not well or she'd have answered her telephone. If you'd like to come in with me—"

"Good Lord, no. You go ahead. I'm afraid me and Eve aren't exactly twin souls. We used to have the odd coffee together when she first came, tell each other when our hems were uneven—you know—but a boyfriend I had—he was a nice boy—caught sight of her and that was the end of him so far as *I* was concerned. And of Eve for me."

"I'm sorry. I can't think Eve would have meant—"

"What does it matter? He'd gone. Keep the key if you want." The woman was preparing to close her door.

"All right, for the time being." Brenda knew Eve would sooner she had it than anyone else. Anyone else in the world, perhaps. In her mind's eye she saw Eve's office cardigan, sagging towards the floor on one side of her office chair.

The woman's door was shut before Brenda had the key turned. Not interested enough even to wait and see if anything was the matter.

Behind Eve's door there was a tiny lobby. The first two inner doors revealed bathroom and kitchen, both untidy, the bathroom showing evidences of a hasty dressed-up departure. The evidence strengthened in the narrow ex–maid's bedroom, where two potential party dresses lay crumpled together on the bed and Brenda fell over a pair of evening sandals. The two drawers of the dressing table were open, so was the powder bowl on top in its pale surround of spilled powder. The bed had not been slept in since it had been roughly made.

"Eve!" Brenda found herself looking down the side of the bed and half underneath it, opening the long cupboard which bulged with nothing but clothes.

She moved to the last door, pausing with a deep breath before pushing it open, but the room beyond it was empty.

Opposite, the narrow sash window looked across to similar windows not very far away, set in a back brick wall to which stucco had never been extended. Even on this bright April day the room was dark, and Brenda went into the four corners and behind the shabby sofa and into the one long cupboard before sinking down into the armchair facing the door, waiting for her heartbeat to quieten.

So she could discard some of the images she only now realized she had been carrying. Eve hadn't had a heart attack or been murdered by a jealous boyfriend. Or girlfriend. She'd gone off on an impulse with James Marshall. Been swept off her feet, way beyond such trivia as telephoning the secretarial agency which employed her or the office where she worked to tell them she wouldn't be coming back.

Perhaps, though, there was a note; she might have whirled back in for long enough to write one.

Brenda got to her feet and walked round the room again, looking this time at surfaces rather than the floor. There wasn't any obvious place where Eve would have sat down to write, no desk, and the gate-legged mahogany table had its leaves down and a bowl of what was no longer fresh fruit on its narrow centre.

Obviously there was no note. And depressingly little indication of the occupant of the flat, save for another jersey over the back of a chair and a mug half full of scummy coffee on the tiled surround of the gas fire. Eve was the sort of person over whom the waters would so easily close.

There was no note in the bedroom, either. Eve had gone off with James Marshall. If it burned itself out she'd be back, and there was no doubt it would help her to find a note from Brenda.

There were some torn squares of blank paper in a kitchen drawer, and Brenda wrote on one of them, telling Eve she would hold on to her key, expressing her hope that all was well and asking her to get in touch.

When she had written *Love, Brenda* she went back into the sitting room and secured the note with the base of the telephone, her spirits sinking by the second. She couldn't wait to get away from Eve's sad little home, but another and more positive means of lifting her depression was at hand. Malcolm. At the other end, perhaps, of Eve's telephone.

She hadn't seen him for a couple of weeks, it was time he came for supper. She dialled his number, and as the ringing cut off her heart leapt.

"Malcolm Newbury regrets that he is not at the moment available. If you would like to leave—"

Brenda slammed down the receiver and walked quickly out of Eve's flat without a further glance round. Straight to the tube, and stopping for lunch at her own end, at one of her usual places. Back in the office she reported her lack of findings to Miss Griswold in the absence of Mr. Smith, still out at lunch, and she had been sitting at her desk for about ten minutes when Miss Griswold appeared, towing a large plump girl with a lot of frizzy hair.

"This is Gloria, Brenda. I have told her you will instruct her in her duties."

"Of course, Miss Griswold."

With Gloria there had entered that curious, instantly pervasive smell of cottage pie which signals a problem to do with personal hygiene. If Eve wasn't back within a week Brenda would be moving on.

When she had given Gloria a sketchy run through the workings of the office she put her most tedious waiting task on Eve's desk and went to see her employer.

She came straight to the point. "Mr. Smith, there's something I perhaps ought to have told you earlier. I didn't think it was any of my business, but if anything's happened to Eve . . . She went out with a man the night of the last day she was in the office. Tuesday. It was a blind date, she'd answered an ad in *The Times*. The man's name was James Marshall, and I think I can remember some of his address."

CHAPTER TEN

"James? It's Monday morning!"

"Yes, Hilda."

"I rang you at the shop but they said you were taking the day off. Are you ill?"

"On the contrary. It's a long time since I've felt better."

"I see." There was no pleasure in Hilda's voice on his account. "You are no doubt about to tell me that your new regime is responsible."

"My new regime? Ah, the dreaded Eve! No, Hilda, not poor Eve, although she gave me a splendid evening. Too rich to repeat, in fact." Why couldn't he grow out of this adolescent corner of his life? "No, my good spirits are attributable to the visit of an old friend from Somerset. Sally Graham."

Mrs. Moxon, listening at the sitting-room door, nodded her head in satisfaction.

"Sally Graham? I don't remember a Sally Graham!"

"That is because you have never met her, sister mine. She was a friend of Angela's from years back, and when we lost Angela we struck up a correspondence." He hadn't known until he spoke how he was going to build on his lie about Sally.

"I see." The two words expressed Hilda's frustration that she could no longer order him to stay in the nursery until teatime. "And you're taking the day off to entertain this Miss Graham?"

"Mrs. Two days I'm taking off. Sally doesn't know this part of the world, so we're going to drive around. After I've shown her the shop."

"I hope you're remembering, James, that you are well known in a small community."

"Sally's staying at the Grand, Hilda. She's my friend, not my mistress."

"Really, James, that is your business." Now that it was a business she had managed to learn, Hilda could let it go. "I was talking about appearances."

"Of course you were. Did you ring me for any reason, Hilda?"

"I'm a bit worried about Cyril, James, he seems under the weather." Hilda's voice was scarcely less aggressive. "I wanted to ask you about those vitamin pills you were swearing by in the winter."

He told her. "All right, Hilda?"

"Thank you, James." He expected the hesitation, and the statement which followed it. "I shall be glad if you will bring your friend Mrs. Graham round to us for a drink. Six o'clock this evening?"

"Tomorrow?" He was feeling generous, but he wouldn't share today. "Or the day after if Sally stays on, as I hope she will?" Sally ought to find out about Hilda at an early stage, it was only fair. Hilda would approve of her, of course, if finding it hard to imagine such a woman taking the trouble to travel between Somerset and Linton merely to visit her brother James. And he was proud of Sally, he'd like to show her off even to Hilda and Cyril. Especially to Hilda and Cyril. "May I see what Sally says and ring you tonight?"

"No need, if tonight doesn't suit you. I've a committee meeting tomorrow. I'll see you both on Wednesday. Enjoy today." The sarcasm was uncharacteristically mild. "Perhaps spending it in the company of a normal woman will get rid of all this nonsense about advertising for a wife."

"Perhaps." His sense of annoyance was mild, too. "Thanks for the invitation, Hilda. I'm confident of keeping Sally here until Thursday. Hope Cyril perks up."

As the receiver went down Mrs. Moxon, her ear still to the door, nodded again and returned at her usual brisk pace to the kitchen, where she stood at the window watching her son mow the lawn.

"Mrs. Moxon!" Mr. Marshall was there, beaming at her. Hardly seeing her this morning through the haze of self-centred happiness shining out of his face. "Last night . . ."

"It went right, didn't it?"

"Yes. I shan't be meeting any more ladies. I've just been taking your advice. Telling my sister that my old friend Mrs. Graham is visiting me for a few days. Harry Venables won't swallow that, but I hope everyone else will."

"Of course they will, Mr. Marshall. That's what I'll tell Michael. And anyone who's cheeky enough to ask me questions." Mrs. Moxon felt her face redden. If there was anyone who might do that, it was Mr. Marshall's sister.

"Thanks, Mrs. M. And thanks for the advice. I'm off now to show her the shop, will I do?"

Mrs. Moxon leaned towards him in a token gesture and picked an invisible speck from the lapel of his jacket. "You will, Mr. Marshall, you will."

Sally had managed to doze off towards dawn and didn't feel tired. She had her breakfast in bed because going downstairs and talking to waiters and waitresses and probably other people staying in the hotel would be a distraction from her anticipation of the day to come.

When she was dressed she strode the length of the promenade in both directions, enjoying the unfamiliar sensation of being happy and excited. Today the blue sky was strewn with small white clouds, but the wind had dropped and even when a cloud found the sun the temperature held up. It was a warm spring day, the surface of the advancing sea reflecting the changing sky in its swaying gradations of green and blue. When they stopped beside it at some point she'd have to paint it, and he would have to get used to the fact that she couldn't go anywhere without a sketchpad and watercolours.

When she came downstairs for the second time he was waiting at Reception.

"Come on out! It's a lovely day!"

"I know!"

He led her to the shop via the opposite side of the road for the full outside effect, and she stood a gratifyingly long time admiring the dark green Victorian facade and long, curved windows.

"Better *Books,*" she said at last, prompted by the discreetly elegant graphics, "than bedlam."

"Oh, Sally!"

"What is it?" Her inquiring face in the bright morning light showed him how she would have looked as a child.

"That's it! Better *Books,* not *Better* Books." He was ridiculously elated. "People usually get it wrong. How did you know?"

"I just did. Perhaps I heard you say it. Or knew you weren't a show-off." They grinned at one another. "And Better *Books* is such a good name. I've started to wish I'd read more of them."

But he already knew she had read enough to fulfill the implied requirement of his ad—although since he had met her this no longer mattered—and that her reactions to their tour of his shop would please him.

As later his interested approval pleased Sally when she sat on one of the folding chairs from the boot of his car and painted the sea.

Lunch was in the country at one of James's favourite pubs and lasted two hours during which they hardly stopped talking. Afterwards, walking, there were long silences in which neither of them any longer felt alone.

"I'd like you to come to the White House for supper." They were strolling along the narrow lanes of one of the villages inland from Linton, peering into antique shops. "You will, won't you, Sally?"

"Of course."

"I'll make us an omelette. I'm not an entirely hopeless cook."

"I know. It's so easy, isn't it, to forget we began with those letters?"

The immediately important thing when they got home was the meeting with Heidi, who had been left behind because of her reserve, sometimes amounting to hostility, towards people she didn't know, particularly if James made a fuss of them. So he stood aside while Sally approached her and she met Sally halfway, butting her nose against the proffered hand and wagging her tail. Even when James ventured to come near and openly take Sally's other hand, Heidi continued to be happy.

"That's all right, then," commented James, showing Sally how much he was already taking for granted. She was about to wonder aloud how Heidi would hit it off with Blackie but bit it back, not wanting to go quite so near, as yet, to putting things into words.

Then realizing she had just taken her turn to forget that putting things into words was the way they had begun.

But neither of them had imagined being able to surmount their unnatural start and behave as if they'd met by accident. James, who had seen himself showing Sally round his house and garden as an estate agent offering himself with his property, found the reality so different he was able to let her share his amusement.

It was after ten o'clock when they finished supper.

"I'm going to take you back to the Grand now, Sally." There was the rest of their lives.

"I know."

By the front door, for the first time, they chastely kissed.

"Tomorrow morning," said James. "I'll have to put in a couple of hours at the shop. Eleven?"

"Eleven."

The next day was as warm and bright, the pattern the same in reverse. Sally painted inland, a prospect of small hedged fields backed by woods and a Victorian folly, and they lunched with a view of the sea before walking with Heidi on the shore.

For supper they had wine and toast and pâté by the garden door, watching the light fade until Sally, on a superhuman conquest of her inclinations, got to her feet and asked James to take her back to the hotel.

She spent the next morning sketching and staring at the sea while he went back to business, both of them lamenting the separation while half welcoming the breathing space. He invited her to lunch at his usual café, happily aware of the message her presence would convey to a cross section of his local acquaintance.

The effect was as gratifying as James had anticipated but cost Sally a few jealous pangs at the evidences of dismay among the female clientele, and a reminder that she knew nothing about James's everyday life.

"*What* am I interrupting?" she demanded as jokily as she was able, when the rather pretty young woman who had stood for an agonized moment beside their table, wringing out a handkerchief and trying not to look at Sally while she asked James what he thought of her latest poem, had wandered blinking and red-faced away.

"Nothing, nothing!" He was aghast at the complacency which had suddenly lost him Sally's frank gaze. "That was just Sophy, I met her at a dinner party and she's haunted my shop ever since. Her poems are unsolicited, and I've never so much as offered her a cup of tea. And those others . . . Hostesses gnashing their teeth at the potential loss of a dinner-party single. The girl in red was served up to me a few weeks ago and I didn't eat her. Sally . . ."

Thank heaven she was looking him in the eyes again. And really smiling.

"I didn't expect you to be living in a vacuum, James. I'm pleased other women find you attractive." She was, of course. But it was time she went home and took stock. "I wasn't looking for a monk."

"I sometimes think I'm a bit like the local curate. Some woman who used to come a lot into the shop actually knitted me a pair of socks."

They both laughed at that, but the euphoria was missing from their evening reunion, replaced in them both by an unstated slight anxiety.

In the dusk after supper, sitting again by the open garden door, James knew he must force the moment of truth. He got up and went over to his desk.

"Before I met you I met another woman." He picked up the papers he wanted and turned to look at her "I've arranged to meet one more. I don't want to see the first one again, and I don't want to see the other one at all. And I don't want you in their company, you don't belong there. Sally . . . Come down the garden." He held out his hand.

The bonfire behind the yew screen was still smouldering. James bent down and pushed the papers into the glowing cone.

"Not your photograph, of course. But that's upstairs." Grinning, he leaned into the shed by the wall. The spurt of flame showed Sally he had lit a long match, and he bent again to set it to the angle of white paper sharply visible in the dusk against the dark tangle of the bonfire.

There was an instant flare, sending sparks up into the navy-blue sky.

They stood in silence watching the white shrivel away.

"It's not such a total grand gesture as I would have liked," said

James as they walked back up the garden. "I've had to keep a letter from the last one so that I can put her off."

"Grand enough for me." She did not tell him she found it rare and wonderful for a man not to take himself entirely seriously.

As they reached the house they stopped on an instant and turned to one another.

"Sally, Sally, Sally! Shall I take you back?"

"James, I—"

The peal of a doorbell shocked the silence around them.

"Who the hell?"

She followed him as far as the hall and saw the two neat-looking men on the step. She couldn't distinguish words in the murmur of voices, but James was asking them in, closing the front door behind them, leading the way into the sitting room and switching on a harsh overhead light.

"This is a friend of mine. Mrs. Graham. Sally, this is—"

"Detective Chief Inspector Daniels and Detective Sergeant Jones," supplied the obvious leader of the two men. He had sandy hair, freckles and a mild expression, but his blue eyes were keen and had scarcely left James while he introduced himself and his sergeant to Sally. Detective Sergeant Jones was plump where his superior was lean, and perspiration gleamed on his high, pale forehead. "Perhaps if Mrs. Graham would excuse us."

"So it's not just a traffic offence, Chief Inspector?" James's eyes were as straight as the policeman's, but amused.

"It could be something quite serious, Mr. Marshall. Perhaps you would like to sit down."

James's eyes flickered, shedding the amusement. "In that case we'll all sit down, Chief Inspector. Including Mrs. Graham. She's an old friend."

"James . . ."

"Sit down, Sally."

James drew the curtains across the vanished garden, then indicated the sofa. The two policemen sat down side by side. Sally chose an upright chair near the door to the hall.

"What is it then, Chief Inspector?" He was beginning to feel uneasy.

"Perhaps you could tell us, Mr. Marshall, if you were in London last Tuesday night, the twelfth of April?"

The date knifed his skull, but he managed to smile.

"I should have been, Chief Inspector, but my appointment was cancelled and I stayed at home."

"Anyone with you at home, sir?"

"No one, no." Something in the chief inspector's gaze was affecting his heartbeat. "I live alone, and as my appointment was cancelled only that morning I didn't make fresh plans for the evening."

"You received a telephone call or two, I expect, though, sir? Or made some?"

"Not that I can remember." He felt as though he'd been running. "In fact, what I do remember is rather enjoying my unexpectedly free evening. All I did was read and listen to music."

"I see, sir."

"So if you're looking for a witness to something I'm not going to be much help." He must act normally, the chief inspector was probably investigating local burglaries, he wouldn't be interested in the fact that James's appointment had been a blind date. "Except by being able to tell you that nothing happened in or around my house to disturb my peace. A bit negative, I'm afraid, but all I can manage."

"Thank you, sir. Do you know a woman called Eve Harris?"

"Eve Harris?" The words came out as a croak, and he had to cough. "I know *of* her, Chief Inspector. It was she I'd arranged to meet that night, but at the last moment she was unable to keep the appointment."

"I see, sir," said the chief inspector again, and James's spine was suddenly cold. "I should be obliged if you could tell me why you had arranged to meet Mrs. Harris."

"I'm sorry, Chief Inspector, I don't understand."

"If you'll just answer my question, Mr. Marshall."

"All right." If he could just control his breathing. He was tempted to say it had been to do with book business, but the chief inspector might already know the truth; policemen sometimes asked questions to which they had the answers. "I was meeting Eve

Harris because I'd advertised in *The Times* for a wife, and she'd answered the ad."

The chief inspector's face flew round towards Sally, whether involuntarily or by design it was impossible to tell. "I see." There was a just perceptible shrug. "I'm afraid we're going to have to ask you to come along to the station with us, Mr. Marshall, to answer a few more questions."

"Questions on what, Chief Inspector?"

"Didn't I mention it?" Detective Chief Inspector Daniels rose lithely from the deep sofa, followed with a little difficulty by his subordinate. "Eve Harris's body was found an hour or so ago in the hollow centre of some rocks along the coast from Linton. Upham way. Somebody'd strangled her. There was a letter in a pocket, apparently signed by you and confirming the rendezvous you've mentioned. It isn't possible after this length of time precisely to pinpoint time of death, but the forensic people put it at somewhere around last Tuesday night. I think it would be a good idea if the sergeant packed a small case for you, sir. You can go upstairs with him."

Sally, insofar as she could think of anything, thought it would probably be out of order for the detective chief inspector to question her while they waited together, and he didn't; he just said he was sorry, ascertained she was staying at the Grand, and used the telephone to order her a taxi. Then stood with his back to her examining a bookcase. At least Heidi was keeping up appearances, lying back against Sally's legs. The only living creature in the house that was relaxed. The room seemed unnaturally bright, like a stage set. And this had to be a play, it couldn't be for real.

When James came back into the room, in front of the detective sergeant carrying a case, he went up to Sally and held out his hand. He didn't attempt to take hers in case she pulled it away, but she reached out and grasped his in both of hers.

"James . . ."

"I don't know what it's about, Sally. I didn't leave the house."

"I know. I believe you." Not just because she wanted to. Her instinct and her intelligence as well as her emotions were telling her he was speaking the truth. If James Marshall was a murderer there was nothing she knew about human nature. "It'll be all right, it has to be. I'll—be here." She felt very calm, far too remote and unreal to cry, or even feel anything.

"Thank you, Sally."

She got up and kissed him on the cheek. Like an old friend, but she hadn't been thinking of the police when she did it.

"If you're ready, then, Mr. Marshall."

"I'm ready."

"We've locked up," said Detective Sergeant Jones. "Except for the patio door." He stood aside, and like a sleepwalker James went over and attended to it. Then he said, "Sally . . ." and looked at her in bewilderment. "You can't just . . ."

The front doorbell rang again. "My taxi's here, James. I'll be fine. It's just a mix-up. Ring me when you get home, I'll be at the Grand." On a gesture from the senior policeman, the junior walked her to the door.

"I'm glad to hear you won't be leaving Linton just yet, Mrs. Graham." The detective chief inspector's voice sounded gently behind her. "I expect we'll want a word with you."

"Yes. Of course."

Sally was in the taxi, almost back at the hotel, when she thought of Heidi and had her first sensation since the nightmare had begun.

CHAPTER ELEVEN

Again Sally dozed towards dawn, but the newspaper edging under her door had her out of bed and running across the room. Her mind had been churning all night, but she hadn't thought of the press. And television and radio. Unless this ridiculous mistake was cleared up, James would be branded nationwide as a murderer.

Her hands were trembling, but she didn't have to try and open the paper, a small paragraph on the front page reported that the body of Eve Jane Harris, forty-two, had been found on the shore between Linton and Upham. And that a man was helping the police with their inquiries.

She didn't know his telephone number—neither of them had included telephone numbers in their correspondence. It was difficult turning the pages of the directory, but eventually she found it and dialled. If there was no reply at eight in the morning he was still at the police station.

There was no reply.

Sally ordered breakfast upstairs again and drank a cup of tea and ate a mouthful of toast at the open window. The weather mocked her, even more blue and gold than the day before. Down on the promenade a little group of people were talking, two of them hauling on the leads of dogs that hadn't wanted to stop. She could just see the solemn expression on a couple of faces. When she looked the other way there was another group. Discussing Linton's murder. But they wouldn't know James was the man at the station. A suspect's name wasn't released until an arrest was made, and before then she'd wake up.

The directory also gave her the address of the police station, and she found it on the tourist's map she'd taken from the reception desk on her arrival. When she was dressed she went downstairs and quickly out onto the promenade, walking unseeingly from one end to the other as she tried to think what to do. Eventually, with one wrong turn, she found the police station.

Inside was a lobby with seats, and a worn wooden counter with a large uniformed sergeant behind it, smiling at her.

"How can I help you, madam?"

"I've come to ask . . . Is James Marshall still here?"

"James Marshall?" The sergeant's manner was all at once reserved. Careful. Less in her favour. He lifted a huge hand from the counter and coughed into it. "I'm afraid you're a bit late, the press conference was at ten. Should be over any minute. Ah, here they are now."

Men and women were erupting excitedly from a passage giving on to the lobby. Several were already crowding under the arches of the two open phone booths and others were at the desk, pleading with the sergeant for access to more telephones.

Sally moved away from the desk, towards one of the booths. The man who had secured it had got through, she could hear him above the excited hum.

"Ted? You listening? There's been an arrest. Yes! Small hours. Linton bookseller. Local pillar and all that. Name of James Marshall. No, no, Marshall. M-a-r-s-h-a-l-l. Jesus, are you deaf?"

"Not James Marshall! James Marshall hasn't killed anyone!" Doubly shocked, Sally heard her voice over the hubbub. So did the reporters swarming at the entrance to the booth.

"Would you mind saying that again? Telling me who you are?" A young woman had a notebook in her hand, a pen actually poised. So did a young man. Another woman. Light from an exploding flashbulb blinded her. She was the centre of a small crowd.

"I said James Marshall isn't a murderer!"

"You've got evidence?"

"Could I ask you for a statement?"

"If you'd just like to tell me . . ."

"My evidence is that I'm an old friend and I know him well enough to know he isn't a killer." The size of the crowd was at least preventing the duty sergeant from noticing the diversion.

"May I have your name, please?"

"I'm sorry . . ." Horrified, Sally watched the crowd continue to grow. Losing the blinkers of her outrage was like coming to after a fit. What had she done? A youngish man near the front with a keen brown face and a notebook gave her a professional smile. "I'm just an old friend. My name doesn't matter. I don't know anything about it and I'm sure Mr. Marshall doesn't either." If she could just get out. "Now if you'll forgive me . . ."

At least the booth where she had stopped to listen was close to the outer door; it needed only a few sideways steps to reach it and be through. Start walking quickly in the direction of the hotel.

"Excuse me, but you can't make a statement like that and just leave it there. . . ."

The crowd was accompanying her, it was agitating round her at the pace she had set. In other nightmares she had wakened before it got to this.

"Please . . . I've nothing to tell you except that I'm a friend of Mr. Marshall's. I know him. He's not a killer."

She repeated herself over and over as one spokesman gave way to another, until they were almost at the hotel and someone asked her if she was in Linton on holiday.

"Yes. Yes!"

"Visiting James Marshall?"

"Yes! I told you, I'm an old friend."

"Were you here the night Eve Harris was murdered?"

"No! Neither was he. I mean, he didn't kill her. . . ."

She still wasn't waking up, the crowd was following her into the hotel, hearing the reception clerk call her Mrs. Graham as he handed over her key.

She turned on them as the lift door opened. "You know my name. No doubt you're about to find out my address. Please let me go now, I've really nothing else to tell you." The man with the professional smile smiled again, and she realized the others weren't hostile either, just dead set on a story. "I'm sorry. . . ."

She must have pressed the button because the doors were closing on the eager faces. Another flash exploded as they disappeared. The lift took twice as long as usual, and when she got out there were miles to run to her room and at first she couldn't get her door open. When at last she was inside she locked the door and collapsed into the chair by the window.

And realized what she had done.

That she had publicly allied herself with a man whom four days earlier she hadn't even met, a man accused of committing murder.

A man she knew to be innocent of the charge. Not because the four days had been time enough for her to fall in love with him, but because they had been time enough to show her, in the face of all her efforts now to ridicule her sense of certainty, that he was incapable of killing.

This was her conviction, and she had the courage of it.

The surge of energy had Sally back on her feet and pacing the room as she tried to assess the implications of her outburst.

First and foremost she had made herself part of James's ordeal. Well, that was right, she wanted to be part of it, and at least she'd kept up the fiction he'd invented for the police, that they'd known each other for years.

' *Thank heaven he'd burned her letters.* The police knew he'd advertised for a wife—he'd told them, and the dead woman had had a letter from him on her, to say nothing of them probably at this moment rifling through his desk—but they wouldn't know about *her,* they'd have to believe what she and James had told them, what she'd told the press. His action by the bonfire had saved her from national notoriety as a woman who had looked for a husband via a box number. Whereas he, as well as being accused of murder, would be known throughout the land as a man who had advertised for a wife.

Or for a woman to kill.

At least, as his old friend, she could stay near him. So long as her credentials were watertight.

Sally stopped at the door and examined it. When she had seen that the lock had no keyhole she took the long envelope from the drawer by the bed and pulled out the contents. She put the photograph aside and with difficulty and the creation of a great deal of ash burned everything else with the short, unsuitable matches from the hotel's complimentary book. Then, matches still in hand, she looked hard at the photograph before deciding to stow it in her wallet behind her electronic library ticket. Not from sentiment, she was making plans.

When she had disposed of the ash in the bathroom Sally went to the telephone and dialled her daughter's office.

It was easy enough to warn Gill what she would see in the media, hard to convince her of her own conviction of James's innocence and that staying on in Linton instead of getting the hell out wasn't a sign of premature senility. It was a further task to win Gill's promise to endorse the new fact of her long-term friendship with James.

When she had rung off on a host of unsuccessful reassurances, Sally went over to the window and pushed up the sash. There were more people than usual on the promenade, most of them standing about rather than strolling, and without dogs. They seemed to be looking up at the hotel, and as she took a long breath of fresh air a couple of cameras were raised. It didn't necessarily mean the reception clerk had sold her out; the press posse was determined enough to stake out the geography of the Grand Hotel for itself.

"You've got a visitor."

The policeman stood aside to let the familiar figure into the station cell, went out and closed the door on them. James and his visitor stood in silence listening to the lock, then the visitor strode across the small space, dropped his briefcase, and pressed his hands to James's shoulders.

"James, this is terrible."

"It is, isn't it? I didn't kill the woman, Charles, I didn't even get to meet her."

"Of course not!" But for a split second Charles's eyes had wavered.

"It's a nightmare."

"Let's sit down, James." The bench seat was uncomfortably narrow, but there was a small stained table for Charles's case. "Tell me what happened. I mean, what your connection with the woman was."

"You know—what's supposed to have happened?"

"Yes."

"The first part of it's true. Well, it's in my statement. I advertised for a wife, Charles. In *The Times*. Because it had been so wonderful being married to Angela. Well, you know that—"

"As your friend as well as your solicitor. Yes, of course."

He could see the struggle Charles was having to look at him in the old way. "I had—three replies that seemed possible." He had just remembered to leave out Sally. Sally! Refusing to think of her was like accepting an injection at the dentist's. "I—I decided against going on with the exercise and threw the replies away." Rifling through his desk, the police would wonder why he had destroyed all trace of Eve Harris. "I saw one of the women, she was dreadful. Tried to seduce me in the car when I was running her to the station." And he was trying not to accept that Charles's face was increasingly grave. "Eve Harris was to be the second. On the morning we'd arranged to have dinner in Hampstead—at The Poet—a man with an overdone American accent rang me at the shop to say Mrs. Harris couldn't make it. And that he or she had rung The Poet to cancel the booking, because of being on the spot. I said thanks for being so thoughtful."

"An overdone accent?"

"Well, it was sort of stagey. Like an Englishman playing out a fantasy."

"And you didn't recognize it?"

"No! Charles, I wasn't expecting to!"

"Of course not!" There was another flash of that terrible, unfamiliar heartiness. "So what did you do that evening, James?"

"Nothing. I did nothing. I was rather glad in fact to find myself so unexpectedly free. I thought I'd watch TV but there wasn't anything on so I listened to music and read."

"And took the dog out?"

"As always. About ten, I suppose. And after all this time the murder could have been at nine. Or eleven, or twelve."

"Yes . . . The body'd been tipped into the crevice of a pretty high rock and a week's too long to be able to pinpoint the time exactly." Charles hesitated. "It doesn't help."

"No, I can see."

"You—one needs such a long alibi. Even if you met someone when you were walking Heidi . . ."

"Which I didn't. Not a soul. I might have, Charles, I often do. But that night, no."

"Did you make any telephone calls during the evening? Better still, did you receive any?"

"Neither. It's in my statement."

"I just want to make sure you haven't forgotten anything."

"In the circumstances I wouldn't forget that."

"No. So there's nothing else you can tell me, James?"

"No. The police told me what's supposed to have happened. But you'd better go over it again."

Charles sighed heavily, laying down the pen with which he'd made no more than two lines of notes. "The booking wasn't cancelled. Eve Harris had dinner at The Poet restaurant in Hampstead with a bearded man of your height and build. The proprietor and a couple of waiters identified your photograph."

"I wasn't there, Charles."

A flash of smile, professionally reassuring. "The handbag was in the crevice with the body. Nothing in it but the expected keys, cosmetics and so on. But as you know . . . as the police will also have told you"—Charles's eyes swivelled—"the skirt the girl was wearing had a pocket slit into the side, and screwed up in that pocket was a letter apparently sent by you arranging time and place of meeting. Overlooked by you, they'll say, when you removed the evidence." Which was how it could have been, Charles Bentley was appalled to find himself reflecting.

"The letter *was* sent by me. I never thought of denying it. What I deny is that I kept the date. Because of being telephoned and told it was cancelled."

"Of course!"

"D'you think I'm lying, Charles?" How could he not think so, for God's sake? But as his legal adviser he'd have to act as if he didn't.

"Of course not, James. I know you. It's—unthinkable."

"Thank you." Charles's eyes had stayed straight on him that time, and James was aware of the fleeting sense of hope.

"However . . ." Charles looked down at the almost empty sheet of paper. "The circumstantial evidence, James. It's formidable. And your defence against it is a telephone call that can't be checked. Unless an assistant took it? Overheard you?"

"Neither."

"Mm. It's still your only defence. So our case will have to be attack."

"What d'you mean, Charles?" All at once the long night had caught up with him and he was so tired he didn't think he'd be able to take anything else in.

"I mean, if you didn't do it—as you didn't do it"—smoothly, Charles corrected his mistake—"then someone else did. Which means that your correspondence with Eve Harris must have been intercepted at some point. At one end. Yours or hers." James could only stare at him. "Good heavens, man, what other explanation is there? If you didn't do it, who the hell do you think did?"

"I haven't thought, Charles. Not since the police came and said what they did. It's a bad dream, you see."

"But if we can find someone else . . ."

"Someone else . . ." The hope was there again.

"That has to be our attacking defence. In the face of what will be the uphill task of getting the police to take their eyes off you long enough to look at someone, anyone, else, the case against you being so—well, so obvious. As I just said, even if you were seen with Heidi, even if you'd made and received telephone calls, there would still be so much time left in which—"

"To have killed Eve Harris. I understand, Charles."

"But we'll do our best." Charles's neat black shoe scuffed about on the gritty floor. "This is tricky, James, you'll have to think very carefully about the people who knew about your—er—enterprise."

"No!" But he was already thinking of Harry, who came so often through the patio doors into an empty sitting room, who had asked him to hand over any candidate he didn't want. He was thinking of Mrs. Moxon and her concern for Michael, and Michael looking at him and looking away. Of Cyril studying Eve Harris's photograph with that nasty lubricious look on his face. Cyril was barely thirty and not exactly God's gift, but incredibly he was the leading light of Linton's amateur dramatic society—James had always seen it as his one hope of salvation. And Michael didn't speak like his mother. . . . They didn't have beards, but that could be seen to, and they were roughly his height with roughly the same amount of hair. . . . "No! That's impossible, Charles!" But part of him was welcoming the succession of images. "The leak was the other end. Her end!"

Charles got heavily to his feet. "We'll do everything that can possibly be done, James, the woman's end and yours. I'll need a list of the people you told about your enterprise, and those who could have found out. It's you or him, whoever he may be." To his relief Charles saw the possibility of being able to believe what he was saying. "Putting things at their worst, if we finally fail to interest the police in anyone else at least the Path lab's at work. If—when —nothing comes up with your fingerprints on it, actual or genetic, we'll try to get you the benefit of the doubt."

"So that I can live happily ever after? Not in Linton I can't. And not anywhere as James Marshall." He had banged his head a couple of times against the wall, and it was aching. "Oh, thanks, Charles, thanks for coming. Whatever you can do for me I'll be grateful. What happens next?"

"You're to appear in the local magistrate's court the day after tomorrow, which is bound to result in your committal for trial and a remand in custody." Charles had his briefcase in one hand, and put the other on James's shoulder. "No point in asking for bail, we won't get it. And anyway, James . . . It could be you're better locked up just now for your own safety."

CHAPTER TWELVE

When she felt it was time to do something Sally ordered a sandwich and coffee to be sent up to her room. The intermittent sounds in the corridor grew into a scuffle just before the waiter knocked, confirming her suspicion that one reporter at least was taking no chances on the possibility of her escape. The waiter was young and reached her intact and shining-eyed, but he had to master a further attempt at invasion when he left. She was still trying to gather courage to go out when the telephone rang.

"Mrs. Graham? Linton CID here. Detective Sergeant Jones. We'd be glad if you could come down to the station and let us have a statement in connection with your connection with Mr. James Marshall." The sergeant cleared his throat. In apology, Sally thought idly, for his temporary poverty of vocabulary. "Purely routine."

"My connection's friendship, Sergeant Jones."

"We know that, Mrs. Graham. We'd just like it in writing."

"Yes, of course, but I'm under siege by the press. I came to the station this morning hoping to see James, and when I heard a reporter telephoning the news of his arrest, I—well, I found myself saying rather loudly that James hadn't killed anyone. They followed me back to the hotel asking me to tell them more."

"Is there more?" The detective sergeant's voice, which had been almost distrait, was suddenly sharp.

"There's only my knowledge of the man. That he isn't a killer!"

"I see, Mrs. Graham. And I see you've led the press to expect rather more than a character study." The voice had relaxed again, but into exasperation. "May I suggest you break the siege by giving a press conference and announcing that you've nothing more to offer? The hotel's full of small suites and I expect the manager will be glad to see the back of his extra guests. Although the bar'll be doing well. . . . Just ring down. And come along here when you've done. All right?"

"Yes. Oh, dear . . ."

"Don't upset yourself, Mrs. Graham. Just get it sorted out."

She'd have to tell as few lies as possible so as to remember them and tell the same ones to the police. And other people. At least, walking a tightrope, she wouldn't be able to think about anything else.

An assistant manager told her distantly he'd been about to contact her, that the situation in his hotel was beginning to annoy the other guests. When she asked for a few minutes with the press in a public room turned private, his manner grew warmer but wary.

"It's the only way, isn't it?" she prompted him. "And the police suggested it."

"The police!"

Of course, the worst words a hotel manager could hear. "Look, I was with James Marshall when he was arrested. We're old friends and I'm staying in your hotel because I'm visiting him. I know him well and I believe in his innocence. The police want me to go to the station and write that down, but I can't get out because all those people downstairs heard me say it. When I tell them I've no more to say they'll go away."

The room immediately provided was the anteroom to a banqueting suite, a space papered, carpeted, and upholstered entirely in wine red and no doubt more usually filled with conference delegates standing about with drinks in their hands. Sally vetoed the suggestion of a table and chairs; she had so little to say they would turn the exercise into a farce.

There were about twenty reporters, who seemed to take it quite amicably in turn to ask questions.

"Mrs. Graham, you believe James Marshall to be innocent?"

"You're in Linton, Mrs. Graham, because you're visiting James Marshall?"

"Tell me, Mrs. Graham, has James Marshall seemed in any way different from his usual self?"

"Certainly not!" She knew James so well it was hard to believe she wasn't really in a position to answer the question. And the anger with which she did so was her predominant emotion, keeping her strong.

"You and James Marshall are romantically involved, Mrs. Graham?" This from a young man with a flushed, eager face, who looked dismayed as he heard his own voice. But the straightforward question told Sally that the reason for James's rendezvous with Eve Harris had not yet been released.

"We're old friends." She had to give them something. "I knew his wife, Angela, ages ago in London when we were students." Thank goodness James had talked a bit about Angela in the lost world where they'd been together. Told her Angela had taken a secretarial course in London about the time Sally was at the Slade. Even shown her a snapshot of a dark girl with an ironic half smile. "When Angela and I married we kept the friendship going. Our husbands got on, which helped." *Keep it simple!* "James and I've gone on being friends, we meet mostly in London, but there's nothing—romantic."

"Have you any more specific reason, Mrs. Graham, for your certainty that James Marshall didn't kill Eve Harris?"

"I don't know anything about the death of Eve Harris or her murderer but I know it wasn't James. Because I know him so well. For me that's enough."

At least she was blunting the intensity. A middle-aged woman tried another tack, not looking hopeful. "Mrs. Graham, did you ever meet Eve Harris?"

It had taken them about ten minutes to reach the erroneous conclusion that she was telling them all she could, and show signs of being willing to release her.

"Will you be staying on in Linton, Mrs. Graham?" The middle-aged woman turned back at the door.

"As long as I can be of some help to James." She realized as she spoke that her subconscious had begun to make plans.

"You're a friend worth having, Mrs. Graham!"

But all of them now were leaving the room, discreetly shrugging their shoulders, exchanging looks. Angry tears scalded her cheeks.

It was no better at the police station. As people heard her name their eyes slid away from her, and Detective Sergeant Jones joined her in the interview room shaking his head and wagging a facetiously admonitory finger. At least, though, he accepted her statement without question.

"How was your press conference?" he asked when she had signed it.

"It achieved what you'd told me it would. It was pretty obvious they found me tiresome, too." She managed to smile, and he met it.

"It's all very unfortunate, Mrs. Graham. I'm sorry you had to be involved." Her rehabilitation as a serious person had begun. "I'm afraid we've just released the reason for Mr. Marshall's meeting with Mrs. Harris—the evening papers will carry it."

"It isn't proved yet, Sergeant, that they met."

"Point taken, Mrs. Graham." The sergeant's face was red as he glanced towards the constable sitting on his own close to the door. "The word I intended was connection. Mr. Marshall's connection with Mrs. Harris."

"I hope that's all the papers will call it. Is there anything else?"

"Not at the moment, Mrs. Graham. And you're free of course to leave Linton."

"For the time being I'm staying on. Which I don't suppose will surprise you."

"Well, no. Feeling as you do . . . I'm very sorry. You're comfortable at the Grand?" The sergeant got to his feet, his smile all at once a reflex, his thoughts clearly turning to his next piece of business.

"Yes. May I see Mr. Marshall?"

She waited about ten minutes in the lobby, wondering with a sort of pain how physically near she was to James, and following the third or fourth ring of the telephone on the counter the desk sergeant called her over and told her she had an appointment for ten the next morning.

There was nothing for it, then, but to drive away.

At least no one was waiting for her outside the station, and Sally decided to hold on for a few hours to her restored anonymity by staying clear of the hotel. She got quickly into the car and set off the opposite way to the way James had taken her so long ago, the opposite way to the place where Eve Harris had met her death, keeping the coast in sight and eventually stopping by a deep stretch of sand. Then striding along it, hardly aware of the constant pale horizon or the varying sea wall, until the sea had crept close to her legs and they would no longer carry her.

The sky was still cloudless, and she propped herself in a dry inlet against some rocks. Was that what Eve Harris had done, in the moments before she died? Before the man who had impersonated James had put his hands round her throat? One of James's hands had touched her throat that one time he had kissed her. Not a killer's hand . . . Sally turned her face to the sun, hoping the dazzle would prolong the anaesthesia which was still mercifully preventing real clarity of thought. She'd be no good to James if she didn't keep in one piece. . . .

When she looked at her watch almost two hours had gone by and she had slept more soundly than at any time during the past two nights. The walk back to the car seemed quite short and she noticed the tiny pyramid of a sailing boat and some green slime sliding down the embankment.

She stopped the car somewhere on the promenade and bought an *Evening Standard.* The extra information was there as Detective Sergeant Jones had warned her, mercifully on an inside page. With the information from Eve Harris's best friend and office colleague that Eve had shown her James Marshall's letter and photograph.

There was no one in the lobby and she didn't have to pause at Reception, she had forgotten to hand in her key. As she threw herself into her room paper crackled under her foot. An envelope addressed to Mrs. Sally Graham had been pushed under the door. Heart pounding she devastated it, tried to read its short contents in one glare.

On hotel paper under the day's date someone called Gail Prestwick informed her via a faded typing ribbon that she was an investigative journalist who had been impressed by Sally's certainty of James Marshall's innocence, and that she believed they could get together for their mutual benefit. *I help you prove your case, I'm part of your success. Think about it. I'll be in touch again.*

The middle-aged woman? One of the younger ones with the obtrusive notebooks? At least she knew now not everyone had pitied her simplicity. And that she didn't have to work alone.

Sally sat down by the window, thinking about Gail Prestwick's proposition and watching the restored andante parade of local people and dogs as the sky merged with the sea. She was tempted to stay in her room for dinner, ensure her privacy, but that would be to ensure too many undistracted hours and feel a coward as well.

At six o'clock she switched on the television. James, illustrated by the photograph he had sent her, was the first item in the second batch of news, and there was a photograph of Eve Harris so provocatively attractive Sally felt a crazy shaft of jealousy of the dead woman James had never met. There were a few quick views of Linton evoking a clutch of alarm that she might be part of them, and then against a red plush background a woman with a pale, strained face was telling a group of reporters that James Marshall was innocent. For a few seconds Sally didn't know who it was, and then after the shock of recognition she was glad of the confirmation that she had been calm and controlled. As she was switching off Gill rang.

"You're on TV now, Mummy."

"I know, I just saw it."

"I don't know how to get through to you. You met a man two days ago the police believe is a murderer."

"James isn't a murderer, darling."

"You wouldn't know, you've never met one."

"I do know." She just managed to say it as the terrible sudden doubt plunged her down into icy depths where, mercifully, she was unable to breathe. Surfacing, she flopped onto the bed.

"Mummy?"

"I'm all right, Gill. I'm sorry I've made the media, you must know I didn't want that."

"I don't know what you want."

"Don't try to work it out, darling. Just hang on to the fact that there's method in my madness. I'm as sure as I've ever been of anything that James Marshall is innocent." She was. "As sure as I am that I loved Daddy." *Oh, Tom!*

"And after two days you love James Marshall."

"I suppose you could put it like that. But that's not why—"

"Oh, Mummy! Please go home."

"No, darling. I've another two weeks before term, I'll stay on here for the time being."

There was a slight pause. "Shall I come down at the weekend?"

"Yes, please." She mustn't cry.

"Oh, Mummy."

"It's all right, darling. But come at the weekend. I'll book you a room. Goodbye."

There was no reason, then, to put off getting ready to go down.

Moving reluctantly about the room she reflected that in forty-eight hours she had changed from a woman dressing for one man to a woman dressing for everyone who had seen the national news on television. She didn't despise herself, this time, for taking care.

The lift was near the dining room and she was alone until she was in the doorway. The headwaiter came forward, impassive.

"One, madam?"

"Please. I'm sorry, I should have booked." One day again, surely, such small things would resume their importance. "I'm staying in the hotel. . . ."

"That's all right tonight as it happens, madam. This way."

It was impossible to tell if he was aware of her notoriety—at least the word she had chosen amused her—but she saw a couple of junior staff nudge each other, and when she had sat down at the table for two she thought the gaze of a number of older residents bore a trace of hostility.

"Thank you." It might have been from administrative convenience rather than consideration, but she was glad he had seated her against the wall, at least there was one side from which she couldn't receive attention.

"The menu, madam."

She was still studying it unseeingly when she was aware of someone pulling out the chair opposite. Sitting down.

It was the reporter with the professional smile, and he was offering it to her again.

"Mrs. Graham, I'm not here to annoy you—"

"You are annoying me, I've had enough of reporters." She should have asked him to go, but it was she who was on her feet.

"Please sit down, Mrs. Graham. If you're still annoyed after you've listened to me for a moment I'll be the one to leave." An elderly woman at a nearby table was looking at her with distaste, and reluctantly Sally resumed her seat. "Thank you. I heard you earlier at the police station and in your conference—well, you know that—and I was impressed by your loyalty and your determination. I thought maybe we could come to some arrangement; I'm an investigative journalist and you said you believed Eve Harris's killer was still at large."

"He is!"

"But the police won't help you find him, will they?"

"Not at the moment." She studied the intent face. "Are you saying *you* will? Why should you? Why should you believe me?"

"You believe yourself, that's obvious to a blind man. You just might be right. At the worst I'll be wasting my time and at the best earning myself a scoop. I'm prepared to take the chance. Will you think about it?"

I'll be in touch again. "I have thought about it. Another of your ilk pushed a note under my door with the same proposition."

He was on his feet. "I'm sorry, Mrs. Graham. And for disturbing your dinner for nothing. I'd hoped to be the first."

He was moving away.

"Please sit down again, Mr.—"

"Matthews. Peter Matthews." He had turned back to the table but remained standing. "You've just said you're fixed up."

"I said I'd had a note under my door. The woman who wrote it said she'd be in touch again, but so far she hasn't been. So I've had time to consider the idea and yes, I could do with some help. Please sit down."

"Thank you." The smile was still professional, but she thought there was a glint of humour. She didn't know Gail Prestwick, but this man she could work with.

"D'you know Gail Prestwick?"

"Gail? Ah, yes, I might have guessed. A good journalist, bit of a hustler. Are you going to let me beat her to it for once?"

"You're here." It was all she would concede him aloud. "Will you want to write something?"

"If we get anywhere."

"We will!"

"Well, then, you'll appreciate . . ."

"Yes, of course. But it'll be help first, won't it?"

"Once you've promised you won't be sharing me with Gail Prestwick or any other reporter. It has to be an exclusive."

"I can see that and I promise. D'you want it in writing?"

"I've seen enough of you to trust you." There was no doubt now about the humour. "May I stay for dinner?"

"Yes, in the circumstances." For the first time she smiled back.

"Thank you." Peter Matthews' smile disappeared. "I've just heard why James Marshall arranged to meet Eve Harris. Mrs. Graham, are you saying that a meeting never took place?"

"I am."

"So what kept them apart?"

"Someone rang James and cancelled on behalf of Eve Harris. But she met someone who called himself James Marshall."

"Who the police believe *was* James Marshall."

"Yes." Defiantly she glared at him.

"The waiter's hovering, shall we decide what we're going to eat?" This time she read the menu.

"You talked about being of help to James Marshall," he said when their orders had been taken. "So what were you thinking you could do? The police must believe they've got a pretty good case."

"Too good to be true."

"Well, then?"

Close, she could see he was in or near his forties, and the boyish effect of the sun-bleached brown hair flopping over his forehead was offset by the businesslike concentration of his face.

"James's correspondence with Eve Harris must have been intercepted by, or for, a man with a beard." *My beard is removable.* "Real or false."

"The avocado?" The waiter was back.

"Here. The melon for Mrs. Graham. Yes, that has to be the only other possibility," he said when they were alone again.

"The only possibility. Someone must have got hold of the correspondence at James's end or in London. James told me what he was doing"—the flash of inspiration joined Peter Matthews' absorbed gaze to give her courage—"so he probably told other friends too. Like Eve Harris probably did. Someone only had to read a letter, see a photograph . . ."

"So what were you thinking you'd do?"

"I'm going to see James in the morning. Find out from him the possible leakage points in Linton. Who he told about what he was doing, and who could have read his correspondence."

"Then?"

"Then I was thinking I'd—well, see those people and talk to them about what happened that night, notice their reactions. With James framed and arrested the murderer won't be on his guard."

"And if you suspect someone?"

"I'd thought of hiring a detective and if he found something taking it to the police. Ditto anything I found on my own." It was coming up from her subconscious as she spoke. "You are saying, aren't you, that you'll be that detective?"

"I'm saying I'll do my best, but I'm afraid we'll have our work cut out getting the police interested."

"We won't try until someone makes us really suspicious." It was wonderful to be saying *we.* "Someone will eventually, with your skills and contacts. And we'll be covering new ground. As you said, the police are satisfied already, they won't even've asked basic questions about what people were doing that night and so on. I won't be able to ask them, of course—well, not in so many words— but I'll get the feel of people and the murderer won't be expecting *you,* you'll find things out. In Linton and London."

"And where were you thinking you'd start in London?"

"There's a woman who worked with Eve Harris. Brenda Newbury, you'll have read about her. She said in tonight's paper she was Eve's best friend and that Eve had shown her James's letters and photograph. You'll be able to find her address and I'll go and see her. And I'll talk to Eve's neighbours, you'll find me Eve's address too. We'll have to work separately, won't we, or we'll blow your cover. And I'll take James's photograph to the restaurant in Hampstead—"

"The police will have done *that!*"

"Of course they will. But I'll be putting my questions a different way, I'll—"

"Sally Graham! James Marshall's in a hell of a spot, but he's still a lucky man. Look, I have an assignment in London tomorrow, but it'll leave me time to start a few investigations into Eve Harris's contacts. I suggest you carry out your idea of finding out from James Marshall who knew about his marriage enterprise at this end, then if possible get to see them. As an old friend I expect you'll know some of them anyway."

"I expect so." She managed not to drop her eyes. "Yes, all right. I might just find something to help *you* start on them. Are you staying in Linton?"

For a few seconds the smile became a grin. "I'd expected to be back in London by lunchtime, but after your press conference I booked a room here for one night with an option on a second. I'll try to get back to Linton tomorrow night and report."

"I want to go to London myself as soon as possible."

"So how about the day after? Friday?"

"Yes! Can you have found out Brenda Newbury's and Eve Harris's addresses by then? Although I'm seeing James I don't want to ask *him* for Eve's and anyway I don't imagine he knows it by heart." Again that shameful flash of jealousy.

"I'm sure he doesn't." It was the grin again. "I'll find those two addresses for you, Mrs. Graham, and whatever else I can."

"I know you will, and I think you might call me Sally."

"Peter."

Across the table they shook hands.

CHAPTER THIRTEEN

"Your visitor's here."

He was expecting her, they had told him she had asked to come. He had been no more surprised at the news than he had been pleased by it. That was the sort of person she was, the sort who would never just disappear, take the easy way, who would always say goodbye. He had tried once or twice in the night to draw comfort from the fact that she could perfectly well have written, but he was too much of a realist to have managed it.

"James."

She had paused at the door, on the spot where since he had had her message he had every moment imagined she would stand, but now she was coming towards him, holding out her hands.

"Sally?"

She had withdrawn her hands in order to put her arms round him. His were round her. "You're so kind," he murmured. "You don't have to do this."

She drew away from him. "Haven't you seen a paper?"

"I haven't wanted to. I expect my solicitor will bring one."

"Then you don't know. James Marshall, I'm as notorious as you are. I told the press yesterday that as your old friend I'm convinced of your innocence. You weren't the only one on the TV news!"

"Sally!" He had just been arrested for murder, and he was as happy as he had ever been in his life. The constable was watching, but had put himself out of earshot. "Darling. Of course I didn't kill that woman, but you've only got my word. The police. The evidence."

"I only need your word. And my own instincts. If you killed Eve Harris I've never known another human being. James, I'm staying in Linton and I'm going to investigate on my own account. I'm so angry I feel as strong as a lion."

And looked as weak as a kitten. She had changed in appearance in two days far more than his shaving mirror told him he had. "It'll be wonderful to know you're here but there's nothing for you to do. Charles Bentley—my solicitor—will do all that can be done."

She hadn't known she was so jealous. "Not as well as I can. As your old friend I can talk to people more easily than anyone else, informally, not putting them on their guard. I suppose I'd do better still if I hadn't announced your innocence to the world, but I'm still the best—"

"Sally . . . For heaven's sake, come and sit down. So in the eyes of the world we're just good friends?"

"Yes, and a pair of them are on us now." But he resisted her attempt to withdraw her hand from his across the battered table top. "James, you've got to tell me who knew about your marriage enterprise. And who could have had a chance to see your correspondence with Eve Harris, and her photograph, even if you didn't tell them. You didn't kill her, so she was killed by someone who pretended to be you, and he could only do that by reading your correspondence. Or Eve's."

"Eve's. It must have been Eve's." But since his conversation with Charles the shock of the thought of a leak at his end had worn off.

"It could as well have been, but we'll start here. They won't let me stay with you very long, tell me quickly who knew. And who could have found out. James!" She had withdrawn her hand to produce a ballpoint and notebook.

"I told my housekeeper, Mrs. Moxon. I didn't mean to but it came out. Perhaps because of Michael. Her son."

"Her son?" she snapped.

"My gardener. I told you, he's a bit—strange. Personally I don't think he's crazy, just withdrawn. His mother's always hoping he'll find a girl who'll bring him out. I told her about me and then suggested she go to a marriage agency about him."

"And she could have read your papers while you were at work?"

"I'm afraid so."

"Her son—is he like you in height and build?"

The shock was back. "He's tall. A bit fairer but with about the same amount of hair, I suppose."

"Could he have entertained Eve anything like you'd have done?

Well enough to take her through dinner in London and a drive to Linton?"

"I just don't know. He spoke quite well. And fluently sometimes, I've heard him when he's got going about some book that struck him. But Sally—"

"Who else?"

"This is ridiculous, it just isn't possible for—"

"Who else, James? Last time I saw you, you talked about your nephew."

"Cyril. Yes. I wasn't going to say anything to Hilda or Cyril, but unfortunately friend Harry told them one evening after dinner when I was out of the room. Thinking that as I'd told him I'd told them. Rather a naive reaction on Harry's part, now I come to think of it."

"Meaning he could have been making plans and didn't want to be the only one known to have seen your correspondence?"

"I didn't mean that. Not consciously, anyway. Sally . . ."

"Could Harry have found himself alone with the Eve correspondence?"

"Yes. His garden backs on mine and we've encouraged a gap in the hedge. We each have the other's keys. And of course if the patio door isn't locked he'll just walk in. But Sally—"

"What happened that evening?"

There was comfort in her bossiness. "Hilda's outraged reaction spurred me as usual over the top and I threw the whole lot into her lap. Of course she pounced on Eve's photograph, which was undoubtedly the most provocative item, and then Harry had a look at it, and then Cyril kept trying to see it from the arm of the sofa where Harry'd put it down without his mother noticing what he was up to."

"I thought he was a grown man."

"I doubt he'll ever be that, but yes, darling, he's knocking thirty. And an accountant in the city. I expect I told you. When mother's around he behaves to suit her, but I gather he doesn't always come straight home at night. And . . ."

"Yes?"

"Incredibly, he's the leading light of the local dramatic society.

It's justified, he's good. He mostly plays juvenile lead, but can cope very well with the older man. Oh, God."

"You've got to tell me these things. Height?"

"Near enough to make no matter. About the same amount of hair, although he punishes it."

"Hair can be arranged. Harry?"

"Thinner than me. Darker." His eyes pleaded with her. "Roughly the same height and amount of hair."

"It could have been either of them. Or Michael."

"No." But the exclamation mark had gone. "It was the other end. Eve's photograph shocked Hilda, she could have led a rackety life. All sorts of people at her end could have seen the correspondence."

"Yes, but if I understand things they'd be people who'd already had what they wanted out of Eve. Surely the person who went to these lengths couldn't have got her any other way. James!"

"What is it, darling?"

"Me, it's me. I must have been in that pile of papers you threw into your sister's lap."

He seized the hand agitating on the table. "It's all right, at that stage, all I'd had from you was a note. You were the only woman, now that I think of it, who replied in the first place with restraint. The others all sent their life stories straight off into the blue. I'm sure no one saw the note. And anyway they were all taken up with Eve." Realizing what he had said, he looked away from her.

"Good! So to your sister, too, we're old friends?"

"Yes. Don't you remember? She'd asked us round."

"I'd forgotten. It seems—a long time ago." They could bear to look at each other only for brief moments. She turned back to the notebook. "Give me her address and phone number, please. And Harry's."

"All right." He reeled the addresses off, then hesitated. "The telephone numbers are in the book in the little drawer under the sitting-room telephone. Sally, if you really are staying on in Linton . . . Will you please go and live in my house?" *And never leave it.*

"Yes. Yes, of course!" *And stay there for ever.* "James, Heidi!" How could she have forgotten Heidi, who had worried her so much in the night?

"Heidi's in the police pound. She'd love you to take her home. If the police have finished in the house I'm sure they'll let you have the keys. When does your term start?"

"I've another two weeks' holiday. And then I suppose it's possible the headmaster won't want me back." Or would welcome her with open arms and get the General Studies class writing essays on the psychology of trust.

"Give your notice first." Their hands convulsed. "I'm reminded to say that during my enforced separation from my cheque book and credit cards my solicitor, Charles Bentley, will dole out the housekeeping. His phone number's in that book. And while I'm thinking. The car keys should be on the hall table." Where he'd thrown them down after he'd brought her into the house, in that other world. "Use my car when you've got Heidi with you, she has her own compartment."

"I will. Does she go upstairs at night?" If she did, there would be no moment when Sally could be entirely desolate.

"If invited. They've let me speak to Mrs. Moxon, by the way. She'll be at the White House until noon, as she is every weekday. Sally . . . Unless—unless anyone read my correspondence, Mrs. Moxon's the only person who knows how we met. The morning after our first evening I couldn't hide my happiness, and as I've told you she knew what I was up to. But she'll play the fiction of the old friends, she's a wise woman. As for Hilda, I've already convinced her I've known you for years. There may be some annoyance that I've kept you to myself until now, but you'll soon disperse that. Anyway, in view of—what's happened—I don't suppose she'll be quite herself. She's been to see me, which I appreciate. It cost her."

"I'll call on her. And ring Harry. Does he know—where you are?"

"I asked Mrs. Moxon to tell him."

"But he doesn't know about me."

"Not as Sally Graham. I showed him my ad and my CV when I was composing them, to get a reaction, but when it reached the stage of replies I went reticent. Now that I think of it, he saved me from being a bit precious in the ad." It was like remembering something from a very long time ago.

"So Harry doesn't know my name or what I look like." She held his eyes. "Unless—"

"No, he doesn't. And he was away at a conference of estate agents the night you and I met. Came back yesterday. But he's shrewd. He may suspect an old friend being pulled out of a hat. I just don't know, Sally."

"Right. No one else?" The constable had begun to shuffle his feet.

"No one else."

"Goodbye, then." But they hadn't finished. "What next?"

"I appear before the magistrates in the morning, and Charles tells me I'll be remanded in custody until my trial in the Crown Court."

She squeezed his hand. "I'm going to London tomorrow. I want to talk to Eve Harris's office mate Brenda Newbury. She told the press she was Eve's best friend."

"Sally . . ."

"I'll be all right. And I'll have an escort. An investigative journalist befriended me last night at dinner when the senior residents were looking askance, and he's going to find me Brenda Newbury's address and investigate Eve Harris's other contacts and go round with me in London."

"Why should he?"

James was scowling, his morale was still good enough for him to be jealous. "He seems to think there's a chance I'm right about your innocence and he's attracted by the thought of the scoop for him when it's proved I am. He wasn't the only one, darling. There was a woman reporter too but Peter Matthews got to me first."

"Sally, I wish you wouldn't—"

"Time's up, madam. If you'll just say goodbye now."

The policeman was looking at Sally, avoiding looking at James. They got to their feet.

"Please," said James in quiet desperation. "May we have one more minute?"

"Make it snappy." The policeman replied to Sally's smile.

James lowered his voice. "Darling, there just could be something in the muckiest of the papers tomorrow. My solicitor sent me a message last night to warn me. I told you I'd met—one other woman, and how awful it had been. What happened is that we had a very tedious dinner and then when I was taking her to the station she asked me to stop the car. So urgently I thought she was ill. But —well, she threw herself on me. I had to get out of the car to get away from her. Then *she* got out and stumped off. I drove alongside her, trying to persuade her to get back in, it was dark. She wouldn't, but thank God a taxi came and she hailed it, I was never so glad to see a taxi. Sally . . . This woman's been in touch with one of the daily muckrakers, I can't remember which, and told them I tried to do to her what was done to Eve Harris. Sally . . ."

"No fury like a woman scorned," she managed to whisper.

"You thought you'd withstood the worst, didn't you? Had your faith tested as far as it would go?"

She was waiting for the icy plunge, but it wasn't coming. She had absorbed what he had told her, and the sickness in her chest was only for him. "It's all right. But I'm so terribly sorry. Shall I ask them at the desk for Heidi and your keys? Tell them what I'm going to do?"

"Sally!"

In the lobby she conferred with the duty sergeant, and a few moments after he had spoken into his telephone a WPC appeared with Heidi on a lead and starting to tug towards Sally as soon as she saw her.

"She knows you," said the WPC, smiling. "We're so glad you're taking her. She's due for a meal at one, but I expect you know."

"Yes." Mrs. Moxon would know. "Thank you for looking after her."

The lead was transferred, and a bunch of keys, and Sally and Heidi went out to the car. When Sally pulled her seat forward Heidi jumped instantly onto the back seat and lay down grinning, and James's latest disgusting news seemed to dissolve into the sight of her stretched glowing and relaxed the full width of the car.

Sally consulted her notebook and her map of Linton, then set off the short drive to Hilda Passy's. The house, narrow and pebble-dashed, had been built in the thirties along with five others, each of them detached at the expense of architectural proportion. Heidi was looking through the window by the time they drew up at the neat gate, but showed no disposition to get out.

"Good girl," said Sally on the pavement, leaning back into the car to pat the dog and set her tail off. "I don't think I'll be long."

The small front garden was neat too, but there was no grass or soil, just a few symmetrically set pots on the pink and fawn paving stones, planted with narcissi and hyacinths.

Sally rang the bell and watched something slow and dark approach the patterned glass door, its outline wavery as if under water.

"Yes."

Her first reaction to James's sister was that she was in a trance. James had talked of her natural severity of expression, but the pale eyes seemed to look unseeingly through Sally, and the sharp-featured face was blank.

"Mrs. Passy? I'm Sally Graham, James's old friend whom you so kindly invited to come and see you with James before—before this awful thing happened." She was muddled over dates, but had an idea it would have been the night before. "I've just been to see him and he's suggested I go and stay in his house. Keep it occupied and look after the dog." The sort of suggestion one would make to an old friend. "I thought I'd come and see you on the way there, let you know what I was going to do." She'd remembered more of James's comments about his sister than she'd realized, she'd almost phrased it as a plea rather than a statement of *fait accompli.*

"Stay in James's house," repeated Hilda, as if she would never again find anything or anyone familiar. "Look after the dog." Life came back into the impassive face abruptly, and in dual form. Native suspicion, thought Sally, was struggling with relief that someone else had the problem of the dog. "You'd better come in."

"Thank you."

Hilda Passy put her hand out to the wall as slowly she led the way into a gloomy, overfurnished room, feeding Sally's fancy that inward visions were obscuring her sight. "Sit down," said Hilda. She herself took the largest chair, bending her body bit by bit, as if it ached.

"I'm so very sorry." Sally perched on the edge of a two-seater settee upholstered in uncut moquette.

"I can't believe it. But I knew that woman was trouble!" Hilda

Passy's face was suddenly, furiously alive, her eyes burning indig-
nantly into Sally's. "You could almost say she asked for it."

"Oh, no!" admonished Sally. "Not for that. Someone has been
very wicked."

"Someone?" Hilda was lost again.

"Hilda—may I call you Hilda?—you and I know your brother
didn't kill Eve Harris, that he isn't capable of killing."

"You and I . . . Why haven't I seen you before?"

"I hardly ever come to Linton. James and I tend to meet in
London. Angela and I were friends there before either of us got
married."

"You came to see James"—the indignation was back, less strongly
—"and he wrote to that woman!"

"He wanted to get married again, Hilda. He and I are just good
friends." She hadn't said it as a cliché and it didn't sound like one.
"I'll be here in Linton as long as either of you wants me.
Hilda . . ."

"He's lucky," said Hilda, and then, horrifically, her face distorted
with the first of a series of long, dry sobs. "James wouldn't hurt a
fly!" It took Sally a moment to decipher the words being repeated
over and over.

"I know he wouldn't. This nightmare will end, you'll see." There
was something about James's sister, even *in extremis,* which re-
pelled the idea of offering physical consolation, and Sally was relieved when she stopped sobbing as abruptly as she had begun and
straightened her shoulders.

"I'm glad you're here, Sally," said Hilda Passy.

Ten minutes and James's preparation had been enough to tell
Sally this was a rare overture. There was unlikely to be trouble
from Hilda. "So am I. And I'm glad you've got your son at such a
time. I took forward to meeting him."

"Cyril?" Hilda's gaze lengthened again, a long way through Sally.
"Yes, he's here, he lives with me."

"I know." She got to her feet. "I must get to the White House
before Mrs. Moxon leaves. Reassure her James is in good heart. He
is, Hilda."

"It's terrible. Our position here . . ."

Words Sally had hoped not to hear, which disappointed her.

"That's the least of it. James is all that matters. The police won't be interested in investigating anyone else, so I'll have to do it myself." She'd intended leaving it until their next meeting, but was unable to. "Hilda, you realize, don't you, that someone must have seen the correspondence between James and Eve Harris to have been able to impersonate James?"

"Impersonate—James?"

"Yes! James didn't meet Eve or kill her, so someone else did. Someone who saw the correspondence." She stopped short of the words *James's end or Eve's end,* but she had a reaction without them. There was no mistaking the shock and fear that had crossed Hilda's face.

And sent her stumbling back into her chair.

"Are you all right? Let me get you some water . . . some brandy . . ."

"I'm perfectly all right!" Hilda Passy was on her feet again, ramrod straight and severe-faced. "I didn't sleep very well."

"How could you have? But try to rest now. Do please ring me at James's if you need anything or would like to talk."

"Thank you. I shall be glad to know you're there."

Hilda stood at her front door until Sally's car was out of sight, anger welling inside her against James for not having married his avenging angel, for having invited Eve Harris's photograph instead. She hadn't of course believed he had killed that dreadful woman, but until Sally Graham's visit she hadn't realized—had managed not to realize—the implications of his innocence. She went slowly back into her sitting room and across to the sideboard and the photograph Cyril had had taken for her birthday. Picking it up, staring at the neat hair, correct features and bland smile, she was no longer able to subdue the thought that although he had lived with her all his life she knew very little about him. And that the afternoon of the day Eve Harris had been murdered he had telephoned her from the office to say he was spending the night in London with a friend.

CHAPTER FOURTEEN

James's front garden, noted Sally's reflexes, unlike his sister's, had both grass and soil. Grass cut square around a central sundial on a twisted grey stone column and giving way in curves on each side to soil almost obliterated by narcissi and bluebells and set with small prunus trees. Heidi had begun to moan softly the moment they turned into the road, and by the time they reached the closed white gates she had grown so restless Sally decided to leave the car outside and take her in on the lead.

There had been no need. Without a glance or a sniff to right or left Heidi jerked her through the gate, and there was a tussle of wills to decide whether they would approach the house via the path or via the flowers and the lawn. Sally won, and looking into the dog's anxious eyes after she had merely fingered the house keys and then tactfully rung the bell, she was too concerned with Heidi's coming disappointment to worry about Mrs. Moxon.

"Heidi!"

Mrs. Moxon's first concern, too, was the dog. Straightening up from caressing her, she barely reached Sally's shoulder. Pieces of wan ginger hair straggled to each side of her small, thin face, but the prevailing impression was of energy and competence. And, decided Sally as her eyes met Mrs. Moxon's, creased narrow by anxiety, potential understanding.

"I'm Mrs. Graham. I think Mr. Marshall—"

"I know." Because James had shown her her photograph, or because she had looked in his desk? "I'm ever so glad to see you, Mrs. Graham. For goodness' sake, come inside."

"Thank you. Poor Heidi . . ." Sally let her go, and with anxious cries she sped away.

"She's better off with you than in that police place. I'd have taken her, only my old cat wouldn't of let me. Can she stay with you?"

"She can stay here, Mrs. Moxon. Mr. Marshall has asked me to move in from the hotel."

"Oh, Mrs. Graham, I am glad!" Extra creases appeared as the mouth curved, not displacing the anxiety. "And I'm not all that surprised to see you. After seeing you on TV."

Of course, that was why Mrs. Moxon had recognized her. She must guard against obsessive suspicion of everyone who could have had a hand in the killing of Eve Harris. And get used to the fact of her nationwide notoriety.

"That was because I was at the police station when the press came out of the conference where—where the arrest had been made public. I heard a reporter telephoning the news in, and then I heard myself contradicting him."

"You didn't need long, did you, to know that Mr. Marshall couldn't of done it?" Approval had now joined the anxiety in Mrs. Moxon's face.

"Not long, no."

"Mr. Marshall wouldn't kill so much as a fly!"

"That's what his sister said." A convenient route to Hilda, and an endorsement of James's gentleness. If she had needed it. "I called on her on my way here. She's—very shocked." Sally hesitated. "James told her we were old friends. As I told the press. The police will have looked through everything here." Mrs. Moxon nodded vigorously. "They won't have found anything about me, he'd destroyed it because—because it had served its purpose. He destroyed everything to do with Eve Harris, too, which won't help him. Oh, Heidi!" Reproachfully, as slowly as if suddenly old and arthritic, Heidi tottered across the hall and slumped down against Sally's legs. "I'm sorry, lady, but it won't be for long." She straightened up. "I'm going to do some detective work, Mrs. Moxon." It would have been prudent not to say it, but the anger that was giving her this absurd courage was so much stronger than her fear.

"Detective work, Mrs. Graham?"

Still desperate to discover guilt, had she imagined the flicker of dismay across the face which was now restored to mere anxiety? "James didn't kill Eve Harris, so someone impersonated him. The police are happy, they think they've found the murderer, they won't be investigating anyone else. So it's up to me."

"Sounds a bit of a dangerous exercise, Mrs. Graham. I mean, if you go to London saying Mr. Marshall didn't do it . . ."

"To London?"

"Someone at the girl's end must have got hold of the letters. Right? And if they find out there's just you between them and getting away with it they could, well . . . Anything can happen in London." Mrs. Moxon's mouth pursed in disapproval.

"I'll be careful, Mrs. Moxon." And in Linton. Anything could happen in Linton, too. As Mrs. Moxon very well knew. "I've decided to go up tomorrow. In the morning."

"Well, just you watch out for yourself. And Mr. Marshall's solicitor'll be looking after all that. Like as not he'll get a private detective on to it. A professional."

The flash of jealousy. "Yes, I suppose so. But as an old friend of James's I'll be the best one to take people off their guard. And I want to do something."

"Which is what I'd expect of you, Mrs. Graham, even though I've only known you five minutes. But what am I thinking of, letting you stand like this in the hall? Come into the sitting room while I get your bags."

"I haven't checked out of the hotel yet. When I left James I thought I'd call right away on Mrs. Passy, then make sure I got here before you left."

"That's all right, I've plenty of time to make up your bed."

"That wasn't why." They smiled at one another. "I know you'll have been worrying about the house, Mrs. Moxon. And about James. Well, of course you still will. But I hope not quite so much."

"Of course not so much. It's good you've come, Mrs. Graham. There's some cold chicken that'll do for your lunch. And a bit of salad. Potatoes and carrots. Plenty of bread. I can bring—"

"I'll keep myself in provisions, please don't worry about that. But I shall enjoy the cold chicken." She crossed to the window. "It's a lovely garden, isn't it?"

"Yes. Michael'd rather work here than any of his other places." Mrs. Moxon joined Sally at the patio door and opened it onto the crisp, bright morning.

"That's Michael?" Sally indicated the tall figure moving in and out of sight among the trees, then turned to look at Mrs. Moxon.

"That's him." Mrs. Moxon presented her sharp profile, suddenly rigid. "He's a lonely sort of a man, Mrs. Graham. Keeps himself to himself. But a woman couldn't wish for a better son."

"I'm sure."

Mrs. Moxon's face shot round, unnervingly. For once it was without expression. "You got any children, Mrs. Graham?"

James must have told her. But all at once Mrs. Moxon had wanted something to say. "A daughter. Who can't understand me at the moment. You can imagine."

"I can. But that's how most people will be. It's what's frightening, isn't it? People read the so-called evidence. Believe what they're told in the papers." The pale face flushed red. "There was a piece in my paper today. About Mr. Marshall and that first woman he met. Wicked, it was. Downright lies."

"He told me it might be in." Thank God he had. "Whoever impersonated James was very wicked, Mrs. Moxon, and wicked people have a tremendous advantage, they can use everything, including the truth."

Wicked. An old-fashioned, uncompromising word. The word she had used in her head since the nightmare began. Not cunning, or violent, or cruel, though what had been done had been all those things. Wicked. Someone James knew or Eve had known. Someone that moment crossing his fingers or thanking his lucky stars. . . .

Sally glanced at her watch. Half-past eleven. "If I tear back to the hotel now I can settle my bill before twelve and not pay for another night. It'll take me about five minutes to pack. What time do you go?"

"When I'm ready, Mrs. Graham, I don't work for no one else. I'll be here when you get back. You'll take the dog out this afternoon? She'll be needing some exercise."

"Of course." There was nothing in the world at the moment, given the possibilities, that she would rather do.

Mrs. Moxon led the way back to the front door and opened it. "I'll get your bed made up, Mrs. Graham. I'll show you round when you come back."

She watched Sally's car out of sight, then walked more slowly

than usual to the open patio door. Michael had moved closer to the
house and was in earshot. She called him.

"What is it, Ma?" Grudgingly he turned towards her.

"Go round to the kitchen and come in. Wipe your feet."

"It's not dinner time. I've things to finish before dinner time."
She saw the familiar mutinous thrust of his jaw.

"I want to talk to you. Go on."

She was sitting at the kitchen table when he came in and stood
in the doorway, ostentatiously scraping his boots on the mat.

"That'll do, Michael. Come and sit down."

"You holding a meeting, Ma?"

"I'm not playing a joke. Right?" She leaned across to him. "Michael, you were out that night, the night that woman was killed
they've arrested Mr. Marshall for. Out till late." They stared at
each other, expressionlessly intent. When she realized Michael
would not react, Mrs. Moxon went on. "I only showed you those
letters of Mr. Marshall's 'cos of wanting you to see what men can
do to find good women. The woman who's just been here—you
saw her!—she's the woman Mr. Marshall found that way. She's
standing by him. Because he didn't do it. Someone rang him to
cancel the meeting with the woman that was killed. Then met her
himself, and . . . Michael!" Straining forward, she grabbed at his
hand, pulled it towards her across the table. "What were you doing
that night?"

"I was in the wine bar, Ma." Slowly he withdrew his hand from
her grasp, not ceasing to stare at her. "I'm in the wine bar three
nights a week at least, you know that. And often on a Tuesday."

"Michael!" Her voice cracked. "You telling me the truth?" Suddenly she was on her feet and round the table, taking him by the
shoulders and trying to shake him, making no impression on his
immobility. "You saw that photograph, and I saw your face. Michael, did you meet that woman?"

Still he didn't move, didn't turn round, and collapsing into tears
Mrs. Moxon laid her head against his neck, her tense arms relaxing
into an embrace which brought no more reaction than her on-
slaught.

"I'm sorry, Michael, I'm sorry. Forgive me, I been so worried.
Worried first that I took advantage of Mr. Marshall and showed

you those papers, then worried what—what it might have led to. Oh, Michael, son, forgive me!"

There was still no response. Mrs. Moxon dragged herself back to her chair. "Michael . . ."

"You oughtn't to have said that, Ma." His eyes raged through her, unblinking. "You oughtn't to have said it."

"Forgive me," she whispered. "Michael . . ."

For a merciful moment she saw that he was looking at her in his usual way. Then he got up and went back into the garden.

This time Sally let herself in. "It's me, Mrs. Moxon!" she called from the hall. Heidi ran at her from the kitchen, tail waving.

"Up here!" Mrs. Moxon appeared at the curve of the stairs. "Just seeing to your bed. You leave those bags—"

"There's nothing to them." Sally and Heidi sprang up the stairs and Mrs. Moxon retreated before them, leading the way into a front room.

"This is the guest room. I thought you'd be—better here, with all the drawers and cupboards empty, like." There was nothing even Sally could find sinister in the way Mrs. Moxon's eyes slid away from hers. It was pure modesty.

But in half an hour the eyes had become puffy and red-rimmed.

"It's a nightmare," said Sally. She put her hand on Mrs. Moxon's arm, postponing the pleasure of James's guest room and the view over low-pitched roofs to the sea. "But we'll wake up."

"I know." Gratitude swelled across Mrs. Moxon's face, and she seemed to relax into it. "It's just that sometimes it comes over you . . ."

"Yes. That's where Heidi's going to help me."

"She'll do that. Now, you've got your own little bathroom just through here, Mrs. Graham, I've put out towels. And I've put your lunch on a tray and taken it through to the sitting room. Michael comes into the kitchen for his dinner when he's ready, any time from now on. His is set out there. He'll make his own tea and he won't bother you, he knows you're mistress of the house."

"Mrs. Moxon!"

"That's what you are," said Mrs. Moxon firmly. "And I'm not

just saying that because of how things are. I must admit I didn't
think Mr. Marshall was going about things the right way, I thought
he ought to be going to a marriage agency, but something must of
guided him. And I didn't think it'd be something I'd ever say again,
or want to, about somebody else. Mistress of the house. I loved
Mrs. Marshall like my own daughter. But the time's come to start
again."

"Thank you."

"You'll excuse me, Mrs. Graham, if I go now? I think the worry's
catching up with me and I wouldn't mind a lie down."

"Of course. Will I see you tomorrow?"

"I come every weekday. But if you'd sooner—"

"Come as you always do, please. We'll keep each other brave. I'm
going to London in the morning, as I told you, but not at crack of
dawn. What time will you be here?"

"Towards half-past nine."

"Fine. Thank you for making me so welcome."

"Thank you for coming, Mrs. Graham. If Michael's still here
when you take Heidi out after lunch, just tell him you're going and
then leave the back door open. He'll come in again for his last brew
of tea, then lock the door after himself and put the key in that
wicker basket hanging in the porch, down underneath the plastic
bags."

The moment Mrs. Moxon had gone, the instant the front door
closed, the house expanded round Sally as a living thing. In a way
it hadn't done when she'd been there with James. Then, she had
learned that she liked it, but not whether it liked or disliked her.
She needed to be alone in it to find out if it was friendly or hostile.

Her room approved her presence, and the bright square landing,
the smaller spare room and the larger bathroom. What was clearly
James's study gave her a restrained welcome. She stopped on the
threshold and didn't abuse it, didn't this first time attempt to iden-
tify any but the most self-revealing of the books which almost lined
it, and outside what had to be his bedroom she stood still, learning
the quality of the silence and its minute interruptions, beginning to
recognize the olfactory print of the house compounded of its own
precise recipe of fabrics and cleaning things and the unique scent
stamp of its owner.

Eventually she pushed the open door wide and looked about her through a sudden haze of tears. Austere, as she had hoped, with a wall of white cupboards and one fine large mahogany chest of drawers. A low bookshelf, a double bed in which for a flash her mind's eye saw Angela beside James before it saw him alone. If she had ached only in body she might have thrown herself down with her head on the pillow, but the parallel pains of mind and spirit had her tiptoeing across the carpet and crouching down at the bookshelf, blinking the tears away. These must be the favourites. Both *Alices*, with Tenniel illustrations. Poems by Byron, John Betjeman and Philip Larkin. Complete *Shakespeare. The Wind in the Willows* . . .

A sound from downstairs made her reel back on an absurd guilty reflex. But she was glad to be brought to attention, to linger in one place was to jeopardize that precious first impression which is so soon lost and so difficult of recall. Sally stumbled over Heidi, spread out on the landing, and the two of them raced downstairs. Nowhere left, now, where she hadn't been before, but the first chance of an exchange of reactions with the dining room, the sitting room, the triangular cloakroom tucked round beside the front door. The sound had told her Mrs. Moxon's son was in temporary possession of the kitchen and so she stopped in the hall, dropping down beside Heidi and hugging her in her delighted realization that she was at home.

In the house where she was going to live.

She wouldn't go back to school, although of course she'd find a job in Linton. And subject to James's approval she'd go and fetch Blackie.

"Heidi! I can't believe it!" She squeezed the dog's neck. She couldn't be happy, of course, but neither could she deny the strength and exhilaration she was drawing from the burning of her miserable boats.

CHAPTER FIFTEEN

"Yes, this is Harry Venables. What can I do for you?" It was a nice voice, the sort he always hoped wasn't ringing him on agency business.

"Mr. Venables . . . I'm afraid this is a personal call, but I wanted to get hold of you right away."

"No problem." His secretary was close enough to hear the voice, and they exchanged grimaces. "So fire away." He knew he sounded relaxed, and he looked it in the oval mirror reflecting the upper half of his sharply dressed body, but his pulse was racing. He didn't want trouble, and now every stranger who asked for him by name could be connected with the police investigating the ghastly nightmare which was James's arrest.

"I'm Sally Graham."

"Sally Graham!" It *was* to do with the nightmare, but his memory of a type of woman who attracted him appearing to defy the world against the red plush background of the Grand Hotel was overcoming all reactions beyond curiosity and suspicion. If only James hadn't come home early the night after he'd thrown all that stuff into Hilda's lap he'd have been able to mull through the whole of the marriage file as well as take another look at Eve Harris's photograph and read up the gen on her, he'd know now how Sally Graham had begun her bluff. "Ah, yes. As shown on TV."

She had known Harry would be the hard one. "Only because I said within earshot of reporters that James was innocent."

"Yes. Of course. What can I do for you, Mrs. Graham?"

She could only get on with it. "I saw James this morning. He asked me if I'd move into his house and take Heidi home. That's what I've done."

Harry's mouth framed the word "Whew!" for the benefit of his secretary. "I see. You're here visiting James, I believe?"

"Yes." That, at least, was as true for a marriage candidate as for an old friend.

"How long are you intending to stay?"

It was his elaborate politeness rather than what he was saying which was telling her what he thought of her. But she should have seen before now that what to her was logic would to him be a cynical manoeuvre. "As long as I can be of help." *Till death us do part.* No fear of that any more, but life could take him away from her. . . . She was determined not even to see it as a possibility. "Look, I wondered if you'd be free to come and have a drink with me this evening? Perhaps on your way home from the office? The people who know James is innocent ought at least to meet."

Of course she would have a nice voice, James had always been vulnerable to voices. There might be some fun to be had in his house that evening, all in the way of defence of his interests. "I'll be pleased to come, Mrs. Graham. About six?"

"Fine." Sally paused. "I care about James, Mr. Venables."

"I'm sure you do, Mrs. Graham." About James's money and house and garden. What astonishing good luck she'd had, the chance to soften him up and then cash in on his removal from society! "So do I. I'll look forward to seeing you at six." He replaced the receiver. "Interesting, Susannah."

"Who, Harry?"

"The old friend James has been keeping to himself and who in his absence has moved into his house." He'd keep her secret at least until they'd met.

"So I won't be seeing you tonight?"

"She's James's friend, Susannah."

"Since when was that a deterrent?"

"And James is mine. I'll see you at nine as arranged."

But he knew he was prepared for anything.

Sally had no more appetite for the lunch she had interrupted, and carried the tray out to the kitchen. The man who was James's height remained at the sink with his back to her, rinsing a plate and a mug.

"Michael? I'm Sally Graham. I expect your mother's told you I'm going to stay here."

"She told me." He turned slightly towards her, to pick up a drying cloth, then away again. His rudimentary beard could be no more than the outcome of a dislike of shaving. But if he'd taken Eve Harris to dinner, wouldn't he now be overcoming that dislike? His hair was slightly fairer than James's and less wavy, but he had about the same amount.

"The garden's lovely. Have you time to show me round?"

"If you've time to look." At last his eyes were on her, suspicious, even hostile.

"I have. Now?"

"I'll see you by the sitting room." On a final glower he walked heavily towards the back door and clomped out. Shrugging, glad to be joined by Heidi, Sally went obediently to the alternative exit.

"Your mother told me this is your favourite garden." He was examining the wisteria framing the patio doorway, giving no impression that he was waiting.

"I like it well enough. There's the new rockery. Local stone. Good to work with. It's raw as yet."

"It's going to be lovely. I do so like alpines."

"They're all right. Mr. Marshall calls this the wood."

"So it is." He was setting a brisk pace and suddenly they were among trees. "It's nice not to be able to see everything at once."

"I take the grass here down to the ground when the spring flowers are over."

They were out of the wood. *Not out of the wood.* "It's beautiful . . . Michael, Mr. Marshall didn't kill that woman."

He had paused with his hand on a tree trunk, and she saw his knuckles whiten. "You reckon?" His eyes, deepset green, stared angrily through her.

"Don't *you*? You know him, Michael, you know he's not a killer."

"Who d'you reckon, then?" There was no curiosity in the eyes, there was still only anger. That James should have been accused, or that he could be considered innocent?

It was as far as she should go. "I've no idea. The roses are going to be good."

"Not so good as last year. That's the soft fruit. This is my compost heap."

And that was the bonfire. Still alive with a thin string of smoke.

Michael picked up a stick and poked at it. "I'll stay down here now, if you'll excuse me."

"Of course, Michael. I ought to go in, anyway, I've more phone calls to make and I'm going to take the dog out. Your mother told me where you'll put the key."

He grunted, his back already turned, and with Heidi beside her Sally went back to the house, unable to decide whether or not she had anything to tell Peter Matthews.

The kitchen welcomed her the most openly of all James's rooms. When she had cleared her few dishes she went into the sitting room and rang Gill, persuaded her with difficulty to come on Saturday to the White House instead of the Grand Hotel. Then found Cyril Passy's office number in James's book and punched it out.

"Charnock, Ellis and Jones."

"Mr. Cyril Passy, please."

"Who's speaking, please?"

Interception at telephonist level, no private secretary. "It's a personal call."

A brief pause. "I'll see if he's in."

A woman, she would tell him. Not a bad voice. He'd be curious. Nervous if he—

"Cyril Passy here."

"This is Sally Graham, Cyril." She couldn't call the original of that baby-faced photograph on Hilda's sideboard Mr. Passy. "Your Uncle James's friend. I've moved into your uncle's house while he's —while he's away. I saw your mother this morning."

"Oh. Yes."

Whether he was innocent or guilty, what she had said hadn't really invited more of a response. "I'm coming up to London tomorrow and I wondered if I might call on you."

"Call on me? At my office? Why?" He had said so little it was hard to gauge his voice, but she thought it was light and rather petulant.

She had meant to keep it for tomorrow, but she couldn't resist the question. "Cyril, your uncle didn't kill Eve Harris."

She heard the intake of breath. "So they've found—someone else? How . . . When . . . ?" The voice was on the high side, too, but that could be nerves from his misinterpretation of her comment.

"No, no. I'm afraid James is still in custody, the police still think they've got the right man. But James isn't a murderer."

The breath this time signalled relaxation. "You're the woman who said that on TV. We've never met." He made it sound like a tiresome oversight on Sally's part.

"I know. I was a friend of your Aunt Angela before she was married. Before I was. The four of us used to meet in London and that's what your uncle and I have gone on doing now and then, since he lost Angela and I lost Tom." It came now quite fluently. "Your mother knows James is innocent."

"My mother's in shock."

"Yes. May I come and talk to you some time tomorrow afternoon, Cyril?" There was no response. Had she gambled and lost? "Easier if your mother isn't there."

"Have we anything to say?" On his dignity, now, the voice lower.

"I have. Cyril, James is important to me. You're his nephew, I'd like to see you."

"Oh, very well, then." A testy concession. In thirty years' time Cyril Passy wouldn't sound much different. "Better make it four o'clock."

"Let me just see . . . Yes, I can manage that."

"Good." No concession to her oblique rebuke. "Four o'clock, then."

"Yes. Cyril . . . I suggest you don't say anything to your mother." Ringing Cyril at his office was a bigger gamble than she'd realized at the start. It could lose her Hilda's confidence.

"Of course I won't say anything to my mother!" His receiver went down before she could ask him where his office was. But Peter would tell her.

Caressing the smooth curve of the banister, Sally ran upstairs to unpack. But when at her window she had found the silver triangle of sea among the low rooftops she decided to postpone it. Placing her clothes in the drawers and cupboards should be a ritual, not to be rushed, and now it was warm and the sun was shining. Shrug-

ging into her jacket she ran downstairs again, clipped the leash to
Heidi's collar, and let her lead the way down to the shore.

At the brisk trot dictated by Heidi they reached it in just over
five minutes, Sally learning the route as she had learned the house,
as part of her future. But since her call to Harry the glorious
prospect had a shadow across it. A word to an editor . . .

It took another five minutes, walking more slowly as Sally began
to set their pace, to reach the Grand Hotel via the parade. She tied
Heidi to a cast-iron lamp post and went in, recalling in a sort of
surprise the distant self who had first looked round the opulent
lobby. *Tom!*

Leaning on the Reception counter she scribbled a note to Peter
Matthews, telling him where she'd gone and giving him James's
telephone number. *No particular news though already perhaps some
food for thought. I'm too tired to come out tonight but look forward to
seeing you in the morning at whatever time you say when you ring.
Sorry about dinner.* She wasn't sorry, that evening she wanted to be
alone in James's house. And she was not in a position to decide the
time Harry Venables would leave.

Heidi's reproach was short-lived, and the moment Sally had un-
wound her leash she was tugging towards the road and the first
gap in the wall. The tide was far out, and the upper sands already
pale and dry under the unclouded sun. As soon as they were on the
beach Sally released Heidi and she bounded away, running de-
creasing circles round other frantically happy dogs, making brief
contact, tearing on. A couple of tests of her attention and obedi-
ence had her running back to Sally on the third or fourth shout,
and after that Sally was content merely to keep her in sight as she
turned from distinguishable dog among dogs to a dot among dots at
the water's edge. The goal she had set them of the curve of the bay
receded steadily in front of her and still seemed no nearer when
she had grown tired enough to think of the parallel length of their
return. Walking the shore every day, in all seasons and weathers,
she would improve her performance. . . .

"Lovely, isn't it?" The elderly woman with the bright smile indicated the approaching frill of sea, then bent towards the black
poodle which, forsaking Heidi, had just panted its way back to her.

"Yes. Lovely."

"Dogs do get you out of the house, don't they? Yours is a beauty." The woman was friendly and approving. Something neither she nor the other citizens of Linton would be if Sally was unable to do anything with Harry.

Brenda answered her front doorbell and found Malcolm on the step. She stared at him in delighted astonishment.

"Bebe, how dramatic you look! All pale and interesting!"

"And you, Mal, you look . . . Oh, you look like you! Wonderful!" She flung her arms round him. "Come in, come in! It's so long since I saw you!"

"Business. You know how it is. But I'm here now, and I've brought some champagne. Get the glasses."

"Mal! What's the occasion?"

"You know I don't need one. But if *you* do . . . We'll celebrate your recent appearances in the press and on TV." The cork popped. "You looked very good."

"I didn't feel good. I still don't. Mal, poor Eve. She was so craving a friend and I never really let her get near me. I knew she hadn't anyone else but I didn't—well, I didn't *feel* it until after it was too late."

"At least you gave her a public acknowledgment. 'I was her best friend.' That was quite a claim."

"It was the least I could do. And the awful thing is, it was true. She'd quarrelled with her neighbour and even her boyfriend had left her. She went out with a whimper. . . . Ooh, Mal, thanks!"

"Cheers, Bebe. And drink up. It won't keep and it's good for the nerves."

At a quarter to six Sally locked the patio door and sat down just inside it, Heidi comfortingly at her feet. She had been unable to walk off her dread of Harry's visit and was postponing her unpacking again, until after he had been. Until she knew what he was going to do.

She had risked her neck needlessly with Michael, but tonight she might be forced to risk it again, she might be driven to her last line of defence.

Attack.

At least this time when he reached the patio door he would have to knock. All the way along the shore and back she had imagined him walking up the garden, but as she dodged about in the chair where she felt rooted, trying to see past the dazzle of the sun on the glass, the front doorbell rang. She might have guessed.

"Come in." Panther to James's bear. James's height and as lucky with his hair, and no other similarity. But a man with a beard . . . If only she could engage a forensic expert to look for traces of spirit gum on certain faces! It was absurd, but nervousness was making her want to giggle.

"Hello, Heidi." The dog was all over him. It was a relief so soon to discover a redeeming feature.

"Heidi's such a comfort."

"Really?"

So polite hostility was still to be the tone. It didn't go with the intrusive eyes.

"Yes, really." She was leading the way into the sitting room. "I've just walked her miles along the beach. It helps at the moment to be tired physically. What will you have to drink?"

"Whisky. Mineral water. In the corner cupboard. Sorry, you'll know that already."

"Yes." She must not let him see what he was doing to her. "Why not help yourself?"

"Right. Thanks. And for you?"

"Dry sherry." She might have won the preliminary skirmish. "Have you seen James?"

"Not yet."

Another slight advantage. "The committal proceedings are in the morning. He told me they're bound to decide there's a case to answer, and that he'll be remanded in custody until it comes to court. His solicitor won't even ask for bail. I gather your local prison's quite accessible, so you'll find it easy to visit him."

"And you, Mrs. Graham? Will you be here to visit him?"

"As long as he wants me, which means as long as he lives." She spoke lightly, but forced him to meet her eyes.

"Capital punishment has been abolished." He was smiling.

One day, when sanity was restored, her problem would be trying not to hate him.

"Tell me." He was leaning towards her. "I'm terribly curious. What was it that turned an old friendship into a lifelong devotion?"

"But you already know, Mr. Venables, that James and I are not old friends." At least she would rob him of one source of pleasure. "We met for the first time four days ago, because I'd answered the paragraph he put in *The Times*. You had a chance to see my preliminary letter, it was in the pile he threw into his sister's lap the night you were here. But you were too taken up with Eve Harris's photograph."

"James told you that. . . ." She had at least driven the self-satisfaction from his face.

"He told me what happened that evening. He put his ad in, by the way, for the same reason that I answered it. Because we'd been so happily married we wanted to be married again. I think we both knew pretty quickly that we'd found what we were looking for. The night the police came, after we'd had two days together, James collected up all the correspondence to do with his ad"—on a surge of exhilaration she registered the lowering of his eyes—"and we walked down the garden and he burned it in the bonfire. A few minutes after we got back to the house the police arrived. With nothing about me for them to find James was able to present me as an old friend. They took him to the station and I went back to the Grand. In the morning I got to the station just as the press conference ended where the police had announced his arrest. I heard a reporter on the phone to his editor and I just—well, I just contradicted him aloud. As the old friend. Harry, in that role I can do far more for him."

He stared at her, the smile creeping back. "More for *him,* Mrs. Graham?"

"Yes! James didn't kill that woman, I knew that after two days of knowing him. As you must know it."

"So who did?"

She was surprised he hadn't bothered to agree with her. "Someone who intercepted the correspondence. This end or the woman's. You must have worked that out."

"No. I hadn't. But I'm working out now that you've found your-self a good reason for moving into James's house. The old friend, trying single-handed to avert a miscarriage of justice."

"Not single-handed. James's solicitor will arrange for a private detective." *So if you get rid of me . . .*

"And if he doesn't come up with anything you'll marry James in prison and keep his place warm for him for the next ten or twenty years."

"Something like that." Could he really be more concerned about her getting over the odds than about the agony of his closest friend? "Harry, James has been accused of a murder he didn't commit. That's all that matters. Forget me. Or better still think of me as an ally at least until we can get at the truth."

"You're really awfully good, Mrs. Graham." To his disappoint-ment he was seeing a possibility that she might be on the level. A moral justification for testing her further would have given him extra pleasure.

"You can't believe James killed that woman!"

"I believe that James is James. My friend, but not, for that rea-son, beyond human weakness. If he killed her, if he didn't, he's still the same man, the man I love. It's as much loyalty as the loyalty you've been telling me you feel towards James, Mrs. Graham. Per-haps a stronger sort."

"But you must know James well enough to know that he couldn't have killed!" For the moment her horror of Harry's bleak doctrine had overcome all other fears.

"How can any of us know what we or anyone else would do in a certain situation if we're not faced with it?"

"But James . . ." The icy depths were opening again, threaten-ing to engulf her.

"Leave it to the police, Mrs. Graham."

"Go and see James, Mr. Venables, and hear him swear his inno-cence!" That was what James had done, she was high and dry. And the loyalty which for a terrible moment had threatened hers was nothing if Harry was guilty.

"And tell me what a good girl you are? No doubt that's what he'll say. And if he protests his innocence, I'll believe him."

A murderer, maybe, but not a liar. Well, it fitted with Harry's brand of loyalty. If it existed. "And then you'll be prepared to consider who really killed Eve Harris? It can only be someone who saw the correspondence." Again the eyes dropped. "Why don't you help yourself to another drink?"

He stared at her for a moment, expressionless, then got up in a lithe, disconcerting way and went over to the drinks cupboard. He seemed preoccupied as he poured himself more whisky, for the first time unaware of her. But guilty or innocent, if he had not until this moment considered the possibility of James's seriously contesting the charge of murder, he would need to start thinking.

"You?" he asked, jerking to attention.

"Yes, I'll have another one." Sally got up and joined him at the drinks cupboard. All at once she felt as fearless as a lion. "Cheers."

"Cheers." Harry Venables drained his glass in one swallow and set it down. Lifted Sally's out of her hand and put it beside his.

"You took one opportunity," he murmured. "Now here's another."

The contact of mouth and body was fierce, close and sudden, and for a few seconds Sally was passive with shock. Then she pulled herself free. "I should have expected that." She crossed to the patio door. "Will you go now? This time take the easy way out?" She opened the door.

"Certainly." She had resisted him, but her instincts hadn't wanted to. Loyalty to James, or to the image she was striving to create? On the threshold he hesitated. "Mrs. Graham, it seemed to me that a female opportunist had taken possession of my friend James. I may have been wrong."

"Thank you." Fear for her new future forced her to take the opening. "Will you give me the benefit of the doubt to the extent of lip service to the old friend?"

"As things stand. By the way, I wanted to kiss you."

With an ironical little bow he had slipped away, was disappearing among the trees.

Her legs were so weak she had to sit down. She thought she hated Harry Venables, but could he have framed James for murder and then been outraged that a woman might be trying to live off him?

Only if the outrage was a sham, a game, a sort of sexual assault. . . .

When the telephone rang she gave a little moan of shock.

"Sally Graham? It's Peter Matthews."

"Oh, Peter, good to hear you! Are you at the Grand?"

"No, I decided to stay in London tonight. What with my own business and yours I wasn't through until late. I rang the Grand and they gave me your new number."

"I'd left you a note. Any joy?"

"Modified rapture. Now about tomorrow." It was impossible to imagine him off duty, but she preferred it that way. "You don't want any reporters but me on your tail, and they're likely to start all over again now that James Marshall's given you the key of the door."

"Oh, Peter, do you really think so?"

"There's every danger, green girl, but I've found a way round it. Ask for a ticket to Haughton Park—ask loud and clear—and catch the ten-five to Liverpool Street. It's a stopping train, and Haughton Park is about halfway. But get off the first stop after Linton—Turnfield—and cross the platform for the Linton–Liverpool Street express. It leaves Linton at ten-fifteen and it gets to Liverpool Street a quarter of an hour ahead of the ten-five. If you're heard asking for a ticket to Haughton Park anyone following you may be content to sit at a distance, but to be on the safe side get near the door, and leave the train at the last possible moment. And if someone else jumps off, too—well, you'll know you haven't managed it. In that case, if you spot me don't acknowledge me. Go to the Great Eastern hotel and wait for me to ring you. By that time I'll have thought up something else. It'll be worth it not to have to dodge my fellow workers all day."

"I'll do my best. By the way, I never heard from Gail Prestwick again."

"I didn't think you would. She'd have been keeping an eye on you and seen you having dinner with me, realized she'd lost out for once. Have you taken in what I've said about the trains, and are you all right?"

She could imagine the smile might have softened. "Yes on both counts. Except . . . James's friend Harry Venables has just been here, and told me he thinks I'm cashing in on James's misfortune. That I'm an adventuress." She made herself laugh but she wasn't in control of the shiver. "And I think he could have killed Eve Harris."

CHAPTER SIXTEEN

"James Edward Marshall, I hereby commit you for trial at the Crown Court on a charge of murder, and you are remanded in custody pending that trial."

The policeman beside him in the dock shifted from foot to foot, but James's feet were fixed to the floor in the clamp of nightmare. Making them walk back into captivity would require great strength and effort.

The chairman of the Bench was glancing across at him, pain briefly in his face. Thinking, perhaps, as much about those book discussions in the back of the shop as about the uneasiness engendered in a small community by the fall of a respectable man. He knew both the other magistrates, too; it would have been impossible to assemble him an impersonal Bench.

The chairman had turned away, was looking now at James's friend and solicitor Charles Bentley standing solitary in front of him. Charles remained silent, head slightly bent.

In tribute to the passing of a reputation?

"That's all, thank you," said the chairman.

On his way down to the cells James was thinking about the hostility he would encounter in the next court he faced. He had been locked up before he realized that his feet had brought him back to prison of their own accord.

Sally couldn't see Peter at the Liverpool Street barrier. But assuming he was watching for her she stood the concourse side of the ticket collector's booth, smiling and waving at the indifferent crowd.

He was instantly there. "That was bright. I thought you'd be all right."

"Thanks for being here." It was wonderful to see him, have him take her arm and walk her purposefully out of the station. "I'm pretty confident no one even followed me to Linton Station. A man was loitering near the house early this morning and pursued me along the sands. In the end I went up to him and said yes, I'd moved into James's house to look after it and the dog. He was very humble and grateful."

"I told you, you'll be taken seriously now, you'll be respected and admired. It's only a matter of time before you'll be asked to put your name to a book which will lend itself to serialization in the *Sunday Times.*"

"Peter!"

"I've been investigating the coffee situation as well. There's a good place round the corner.

"So you think you've found your man?" he asked as soon as they had sat down.

"Oh, I don't know. At the moment I just feel I'd like it to be Harry Venables and that temperamentally he'd fit. But James's gardener Michael and his nephew Cyril aren't exactly aglow with humanity, either, and they had their chances. Cyril and his mother —James's half sister—knew about Eve, and Michael's mother, Mrs. Moxon, is James's housekeeper. I'm going to see Cyril at his city office at four o'clock this afternoon, and I saw his mother yesterday."

"And?"

"Hilda was in a daze. Mrs. Moxon told me to look out for London. Michael was very angry, but I don't know if that was at the idea of James's guilt or his innocence. And he's the sort of man who could be angry all the time. At least according to James that's the extent of the Linton field. What about you, did you manage—"

"I've got Eve Harris's and Brenda Newbury's addresses, and I've done some preliminary scouting round their home grounds. Eve lives—lived—in an old house in Kilburn divided up into what they call flatlets. One of those places with rows of bells. There were two people I recognized prowling about so I thought I'd wait until the heat was off before moving in. Anyway, I'd hardly have been welcomed just now."

"I'll go, I'll ring one of the bells and say I was a friend of Eve's.

There's a risk of course that someone might remember me from my TV debut, but if they do I can come clean without any damage, can't I?"

"As long as you say you're meeting a friend who knows where you are." His smile was bracing. "I'm not trying to frighten you, Sally, and if your murderer tried to hurt you he'd be proving your case as well as bringing the police down on him rather than just one woman no one will listen to. Well, hardly anyone. I'm only saying it's a sensible precaution, to tell everyone you speak to about James Marshall that someone knows your whereabouts."

"Yes . . ." For the first time her anger didn't feel like sufficient protection.

"I think with Brenda Newbury you might tell the truth straight off, say who you are and that you don't believe James Marshall killed Eve Harris. She lives in a mansion block in Kensington, just off the High Street opposite Holland Park. Got home from work last night at six o'clock."

"Oh, Peter, you're wonderful!" She was over the shock. "You didn't speak to her?"

"There wasn't time to set anything up. Nor to find out about her and Eve's office setup. But she'll surely tell you about that, there's no reason for her not to."

"So how d'you suggest I do things?"

"You still want to go to that Hampstead restaurant?"

"Yes!"

"Then I suggest we hang on here for a snack, that stuff on the counter looks as good as the coffee and I don't suppose you did much with your breakfast. Then we'll take a taxi to The Poet while the staff's still rallied for lunch and I'll drop you off. There are other things I'll have to do today, but I'll try to manage some work on the Harris case as well while you're doing yours. From Hampstead if I were you I'd go on to Kilburn; someone in that house is sure to be retired and at home. That should allow you time to get to the city for your appointment with Cyril. Brenda Newbury appears to get home at six, as I said, so you'll have plenty of time to go on to Kensington. Here are the addresses." He handed the neatly typed slip across the table. "I'll be waiting for you from half-past six in the Royal Garden Hotel. How does that sound?"

"Wonderful. The only gap is the address of Cyril's office, he put the phone down before I could ask him. Charnock, Ellis and Jones in the city."

"That's child's play."

She had it before they left, from the first volume of the café's telephone directory and Peter's street map. He dropped her with another bracing smile among the fresh-leaved trees of Hampstead village, and as she stood alone on the pavement she was aware again of the fine day she had met early on Linton sands with Heidi. The clear blue sky and warm sun which had been the serene setting for everything that had happened since her arrival at the seaside. James would see it again for a few minutes today, when they took him from the police cells into prison.

A man with a beard . . .

"Yes, that is the man." The proprietor of The Poet, prised with some difficulty out of his busy restaurant, looked up exasperated from a brief glance at Sally's snapshot.

"The man in the photograph the police showed you, or the man who was here?"

"You want to play games with me, madame? It is the same man, of course, the man who was here with the woman, the man whose picture the police showed me. The same picture as this. Now if you will excuse me, I have many clients—"

"Mr. Andropoulos, you're *sure* this photograph—the police photograph—is of the man who was here that night?"

The dark eyes flashed. "You are suggesting that I tell a lie, madame?"

"Of course not, Mr. Andropoulos. Please, I'm suggesting merely that one man with a beard on a casual glance could look very like another man of roughly the same height and hair. I know the man who came to your restaurant that night was very like this photograph. But are you absolutely convinced it's the same man?"

She watched the certainty fade from the proud face, reassert itself, waver again. Mr. Andropoulos shrugged. Smiled.

"Look, madame, a man with a beard comes to my restaurant with a fine-looking lady who has a lot of red hair. Later a lady with a lot of red hair is strangled. The police tell me it is the same lady.

Show me a picture of a man with a beard. The same man, it must be."

"It must have been the same man who killed the woman, but was it the man in this photograph? You remembered the woman was with a bearded man, the photograph was what you expected to see. If you'd seen it on a street hoarding, in a magazine, nothing to do with the couple who had dinner here, would you have said, 'Ah, there's the man who came to my restaurant?' "

"A man with a beard? You are joking, madame."

"No. I'm making a point which you've just proved for me." And with his open smile Mr. Andropoulos had also proved that no one had bribed or frightened him into his initial certainty over James's photograph. He just hadn't looked properly at the man with Eve Harris, and then he had seen what the police expected him to see.

It was the same with the three members of staff whom the proprietor, his smile permanently faded, was eventually persuaded to bring out to speak to her.

More shrugging. "How could it be anyone else, madame?"

"There was nothing unusual about him? I mean—did he have all his fingers? Two ears? A foreign accent?" In an eager rush. "Did he smoke?"

There had been nothing memorable about Eve Harris's escort beyond his beard. And no one remembered whether or not he had smoked.

She took a taxi to Kilburn rather than two long tube rides, lamenting the lack of Peter to complain to about indifferent, lazy men shrugging their shoulders, and trying to believe she'd discovered something significant. The Victorian house which had been Eve's last address had the sort of dark green shrubberied garden where the sun never seems to reach. Rhododendron leaves flicked her face as she went with eyes down up the cracked mossy path. There was no reply of course from flat number six. Or number five. The third try, at number seven—designated Ms. Thompson —elicited a sharp crack and then a tired female voice.

"If you're a reporter, will you please go away?"

"I'm not a reporter, I'm a friend of Eve Harris's. I'd be very grateful for a word with you."

"A friend of Eve's? That's interesting." The sarcasm sounded tired, too. "What's your name?"

"Jessie Shakeshaft." She had it ready, wondering where in her past it had come from.

"Are you on your own?"

In bedsitter land the self-protective question was probably reflex even where one's neighbour hadn't been murdered.

"Yes."

"Oh, come on up," said the voice after a pause. "Two flights of stairs."

There was a bee-like buzz, and she entered a dark, narrow hall shot through with the rich colours of the front-door glass. A woman who had been pretty, fair hair untidy and wearing a shiny pink housecoat, was standing at the top of the second steep flight.

"Get your breath back." She appraised Sally while she did. "You'd better come in," she said as Sally moved tentatively forward. "Excuse the mess, I've been ill."

"I'm so sorry. . . ."

There was an immediate stale smell, and the telephone in the tiny hall wore a film of dust. Ms. Thompson led the way into a small, crowded sitting room.

"Sit down."

Dust rose from an armchair as Ms. Thompson removed a tall pile of boxes. Gingerly Sally sat. There was more dust from the narrow sofa as Ms. Thompson flopped heavily on to it.

"It's days since I've been in here." And in here was a television set. Ms. Thompson didn't give the impression of being currently a two-set woman. "So you're a friend of Eve's?" She was looking at Sally properly for the first time since her initial gaze. Still incurious, not feeling she'd seen her somewhere before.

"Yes. From way back. I haven't seen her for ages, but I once knew her well and when I read . . . I just couldn't believe it. I had to be in London today and I couldn't resist coming to see where she'd lived and—well, seeing if there was anyone here who could tell me anything about her in the last few years. Did you know her well, Mrs. Thompson?" There was a winking ring on the wedding finger, so large it was impossible to see if it covered a plain circle. Sally imagined Ms. Thompson pushing it on whenever her bell rang, as a substitute for getting dressed.

"Not well. We used to see one another a bit when she first came here. Three or four years ago now, I suppose. She was doing modelling jobs then, but they got a bit thin on the ground and she brushed up her shorthand and typing." Ms. Thompson paused, showing eight partially red nails as she clasped her hands and leaned forward. "Frankly, I always thought poor Eve was a bit of a mess." The sun, suddenly clearing the window frame, illuminated the complexity of foodstains on the lapels of Ms. Thompson's housecoat and set Sally struggling against an alarming and unfamiliar desire to giggle. "She kept meeting mister right and then finding she'd made a mistake and he was mister creep. That didn't affect me so long as she found her own men—I used to offer coffee and sympathy when required, which was pretty regularly—but after she'd met one of mine on the landing and helped herself to him I didn't want to know. Sorry if I'm making things worse for you, but that was Eve Harris A.D. nineteen-ninety."

"It's all right, I'd rather have the truth as people see it. So you didn't know much about her life when she—when she died?"

"I didn't know anything."

"Not even about her answering that ad in *The Times?*"

"Not even that. Oh, three years ago after one of the mister creeps she was talking about going to a marriage agency. But at that stage it was only talk."

"How long since you backed off?"

"Twelve months? Fifteen? I don't know. Have a drink?"

"No, thanks, a friend dropped me off here and I said I wouldn't be long." The bored face didn't change. "Would you know if she was friendly with anyone else in the house?"

"I might if there was anyone likely. As it is, everyone else in the house is an elderly widow or a middle-aged spinster. Not Eve's sort of thing at all. Or mine, for that matter, but I'm not dependent on my neighbours." Sally saw a gleam of defiance in the sleepy eyes.

"Obviously Eve wasn't, either. Did you notice her visitors?" She had noticed the spyhole in Ms. Thompson's front door.

"Visitors? The last few weeks I didn't even see a man on his way up to her. Before then there was a stuffed shirt used to come home with her occasionally." Ms. Thompson paused. "Well, once a week, actually. No reason for me not to tell you, if I hear someone on the stairs I go and squint through my spyhole. Not just nosy, if it's going to be for me I might as well give myself the chance of getting my expression right."

"Of course. So would I," encouraged Sally. "Obviously you don't know the stuffed shirt's name. What did he look like?"

"Little fellow, hardly up to her shoulder. Hair arranged to hide the bald spots. I tell you, old Eve was scraping the barrel." Suddenly the chipped red nails were fanned out under Ms. Thompson's eyes, which stared over them at Sally large and shocked. "God, she didn't deserve it, though. Not *that.*" It seemed this was the first time Ms. Thompson had really considered the nature of Eve Harris's passing. "For heaven's sake have a drink. I'm going to."

"No thanks, really. But thanks for asking me in and being so helpful."

They were on their feet, Ms. Thompson swaying towards a whisky bottle on a small sideboard. "There was a woman from Eve's office on TV." With the bottle in her hand she turned round. "Saying she was her best friend." So Sally had been even luckier than she'd thought not to have been recognized. "You ought to go and see her, the police'll tell you how."

"You don't remember where Eve worked?"

"You're joking. Eve changed jobs as often as she changed boyfriends." Sally thought the shudder was involuntary. "Cheers! You're sure?" Ms. Thompson waved the bottle.

"Quite sure. But thanks again." Sally led the way to the front door, Ms. Thompson trailing behind her, glass in hand.

"Sorry to speak ill of the dead. Oh, my God . . . It's awful, isn't it?"

Sally had ceased to be aware of the staleness of the flat, but the air on the landing was obtrusively fresh.

Out on the pavement it was even better, and she stood gulping it and wondering if Ms. Thompson and The Laurels were as innocent as they seemed.

CHAPTER SEVENTEEN

"I really don't know what we have to say to one another, Mrs. Graham."

There was nothing yet for Cyril Passy to be indignant about, but he was ready. Passing him in the street Sally would have recognized him from his mother's photograph, but the expression in the live face was very different. Suspicious, defensive, as it had been from the moment he had joined her in the interview room so fatly upholstered she had to brace her legs not to be bounced out of her seat. The defensiveness, of course, could be no more than chagrin at being without a private office in which to receive her, at the barrier between them being no more than a low coffee table carrying a tray of coffee. And it could be fear. This, though, might not be of significance: she already saw James's nephew as a man who would be afraid of things unless and until it was proved to his satisfaction that they offered him no harm.

At thirty he had an incipient paunch and a middle-aged manner. And he was as tall as James and with almost as much brown hair.

"Not in the normal way, perhaps. But as things are . . ."

"You mean because Uncle James has disgraced us?"

His indignation seemed about to break through. Hers did.

"I mean because your Uncle James has been wrongfully charged with murder! Are you telling me you believe he killed that woman?"

"He took her to a restaurant that night, drove her to Linton. His letter confirming the appointment was found on her body. One has to believe it."

She was shaking. "You should know your Uncle James is incapable of killing!"

"How can I know that?" For a moment he looked genuinely bewildered. "I would never have imagined, of course . . . But the police don't arrest people unless they have a watertight case. It's terrible, but I'm afraid we have to accept—"

"Timothy Evans? James Hanratty?" She crashed her coffee cup into its saucer.

"Oh dear, Mrs. Graham." Now he was shocked and prim; her fire hadn't so much as licked at him. "I'm afraid this business has upset you. I know you're a friend of Uncle James's—"

"Yes!"

"But I'm his nephew, I'm family, it's far worse for me and for mother but we're managing to keep calm."

"Your mother's in shock."

"At the moment, yes, but she'll soon be all right."

"You think so? She knows James is innocent."

"She can hardly know that, Mrs. Graham. Any more than you can. Look, when you've had time to get used to what has happened—"

"As James didn't kill Eve Harris, someone else did. Someone who had access to the correspondence between them. Her end, or his."

She had at last caught the pale eyes, and held them while the soothing veneer shrivelled off the face. Indignation quickly replaced it, but on a throb of triumph Sally saw that one veneer had merely been exchanged for another.

To cover panic.

"Really, Mrs. Graham! *I* saw that correspondence! That is, I saw the photograph of—of the victim. I didn't actually read the letters, although goodness knows Uncle James threw them into my mother's lap. Very uncontrolled and strange, I thought at the time. And I've thought of it since, I've—"

"I've thought that perhaps you went back for another look. That perhaps you took the correspondence"—on a supreme effort she edged away from the ultimate accusation—"for a joke. Showed it to someone who made a note of it." The eyes now were bulging, the breathing was heavy and the face was red. If he had a stroke . . . And if she lost Hilda . . . "I'm only pointing out what *could* have happened, of course. The circumstantial evidence is strong enough to prevent the police from even glancing in any other direction—I admit that—but there are a number of people who could have got their hands on the correspondence. Eve Harris's end as well as James's."

"Wishful thinking, I'm afraid, Mrs. Graham." Cyril Passy was in control again, his face almost back to its normal putty colour, but there was a tic at work under one eye, and his hands were twitching on his knees. With a pang she saw that the hands were like James's hands. Perhaps, to people who didn't know either of them, there was a family likeness.

"Don't you wish it to be true, Cyril?"

"Ideal solution for an ideal world, eh? I'm afraid things don't work out like that."

She thought she had summed him up, but she had underestimated his complacency and his coldness of heart, believing even he would seize on her offer of a murderous stranger in place of his uncle. But James was guilty in his nephew's eyes before he had been tried, with the weight of the Establishment against him. Unless, of course, Cyril was the guilty one and saw James as his most reliable cover. Either way he was a species of monster.

"You were quite right, we don't have anything to say to one another." She was on her feet. The smell of the new upholstery was overwhelming. "I hope your mother will feel better soon. I'll go and see her tomorrow."

"Please don't upset her." Cyril drained his coffee cup before rising. "I'm helping her to do what I've done, and resign herself to the facts."

"The facts . . ." She stared at him, now, with no further plea in her face, and for a moment saw panic again in his as he realized she was beyond his influence.

"It's worse for me!" It was almost a whine. "For mother! I mean, he's family!"

"Of course. Yes. You have to worry what the neighbours will think. To say nothing of your employers. I hope it doesn't affect your career."

"It could. Bad blood and all that."

"Oh, I hope not." By now she was hardly surprised he had missed her sarcasm. It was as easy to believe him guilty as so disgustingly innocent. "Well, goodbye."

"Goodbye."

But she was aware of a reluctance in him to bring their bizarre tête-à-tête to an end.

"Mrs. Graham." He turned with his hand on the door, as she had half expected.

"Yes?"

"When I visit Uncle James's house I'm *always* with mother."

This time she let the giggles rip, in a ladies' room two floors down.

On the ground floor she found a telephone and rang Mrs. Moxon's number. She was about to hang up when Mrs. Moxon answered, breathless.

"I was in the garden, Mrs. Graham, but Michael was in the house and so I didn't come in, I just waited to hear the ringing stop, if you see what I mean, but it didn't. So then I started to run, didn't I? He's still sitting in his chair staring into space as if he wasn't hearing or seeing. It worries me, but I suppose I asked for it. He . . . we had a bit of an argument yesterday. I'm sorry to keep you waiting. Everything all right?"

"Everything's fine, Mrs. Moxon. I just wanted to find out if you were coping with the animals and to thank you again for taking Heidi tonight." And to give herself a seaside break. "I still don't know just when I'll be back, so your having Heidi makes life a lot easier. I hope you're managing."

"We're managing fine, Mrs. Graham. It wasn't ever that puss is exactly bothered by Heidi being here, it's just that if I don't keep an eye on him he's liable to go up to the poor dog all friendly like, and then lash out at her. It's a nasty trait in him, but you can't do nothing about it with animals. It's the dog's eyes I'm worried about. I'm shutting puss in the kitchen tonight, he's got the cat door, he'll do all right." How was Blackie doing? Sally noted with interest that her pang was confined precisely to her cat, not spilling over onto any other area of her life as a widowed schoolteacher. "At least Michael's taken Heidi for a long walk, she's nice and tired."

"That's good of him. I'll see you and Heidi in the morning, then." She hesitated. "I hope Michael will be all right." And that she wasn't responsible for what was worrying Mrs. Moxon.

She heard the deep sigh. "I don't know, Mrs. Graham, I really don't know. Now, you just take care of yourself."

"I will, Mrs. Moxon."

But how could she? Looking along the stretch of empty corridor Sally shivered.

She wished Peter was with her in the small café low in the lee of Cyril's office building, where she drank a pot of black coffee and couldn't stop looking at her watch, although when she sat down there was still an hour and a half to go before Brenda Newbury could be expected to arrive home from work.

Brenda Newbury. The last unexplored possibility, and the only person who had admitted really reading the correspondence between Eve Harris and James. Admitted to the nation, there was no going back on that. And admitted to being Eve's best friend, although that could have been an emotional reaction to Eve's death; she'd also said they'd never met outside the office.

Which was probably true, Peter could check on it, but there would be opportunities in an office for surreptitious looks into other people's drawers and cupboards. Sally had never worked in one, but if a staff room was anything to go by . . . And if the two women were in a room on their own, there would be times when one of them was in sole possession. After showing Brenda James's photograph and letters Eve might have shoved them into a drawer, watched by Brenda, before answering the summons of authority.

But to whom would Brenda offer James's identity?

Surely not one of her own boyfriends.

A brother?

She was being absurd, but it would be so easy to find out if Brenda Newbury had a brother that she'd do so, keep her promise to herself to follow every lead however unlikely before hiring a detective.

What she really wanted from Brenda was information about Eve's random life. About who else could have seen James's letter and photograph.

James's photograph, realized Sally suddenly. Not Eve's. All there had been of Eve at her end of the correspondence was her name and address on an envelope. It was only in Linton that Eve's photograph had waited like an unexploded bomb. In London the photograph had been of James.

A photograph to show a man how James could be impersonated. But none to show him that an impersonation would be worth his while. Sally had seen the sexual promise of Eve's photograph on television, and without the stimulus of it the motive for impersonating James would have been no more than the perverse appeal of an outrageous opportunity, or a penchant for practical jokes.

Which made it so much more likely Eve's killer had come from Linton. Where three men had seen her photograph and didn't need to see one of James to know what he looked like.

Sally slumped at the café table, exhausted and depressed. If she'd realized the significance of Eve's photograph earlier she wouldn't have built up a head of excitement at the prospect of meeting Brenda Newbury and be feeling it now draining out of her. London suspects had never been more than shadows behind Brenda, but they had been there, all day they had supplied her with adrenalin.

There was still an hour to go, but she needed to move. She wanted to ring Gill, but the conversation they had had the day before had given them both more pain than pleasure, and today she needed to conserve her strength. Anyway, in the end she hadn't told Gill she was coming to London.

She took the Circle Line tube to Kensington High Street, then walked to Holland Park and looked at spring flowers and peacocks, trying to rekindle her sense of purpose.

At ten past six she recrossed the High Street and went into the red-brick block of mansion flats with beige stucco mouldings over the cavernous entrance and round the windows where Brenda Newbury lived. Up two flights of stone stairs with the handrail almost twisting back on itself before rising.

Waiting after the yelp of the bell she was so tired she had to lean against the wall. . . .

The door of the flat was open and the tall, slim woman she'd seen fleetingly on television, dark-haired, white-faced, very plainly dressed but somehow elegant, was standing staring at her. Through her.

"Miss Newbury?"

"Yes." There was no answering question in the quiet voice.

"I'm Sally Graham. A friend of James Marshall, who—who's been arrested for the murder of Eve Harris. I wonder if I could talk to you for a few minutes about Eve?" Brenda Newbury's deep-set eyes were on her now, but there was still no reaction in them. "Miss Newbury? You know, you oughtn't to have opened the door like that, you should have put the chain on while you had a look at me."

"I've got a spyhole. You looked respectable." No hint of a smile. "You'd better come in."

"Thank you. I hope I haven't come at a difficult time, a friend just dropped me off—"

"Oh, no."

Brenda Newbury, her elegance confirmed by her walk, was leading the way into a large, square room, well but sparsely furnished and so light after the gloomy stairwell and the dark, narrow hall Sally was dazzled. But as her eyes adjusted she saw through the bay window that grey cloud was moving across the blue.

"I'm afraid the place is rather messy. I've been busy and I haven't had time to clean or tidy it." Brenda Newbury's voice would have been attractive if there had been some expression in it.

"It's a nice room," said Sally diplomatically. There weren't enough belongings in it to make it really untidy, but the carpet needed sweeping and on the darker surfaces there was a film of dust.

"Sit down."

No dust rose from the sofa, but Brenda Newbury's neglect of her surroundings might not be the habitual neglect of a Ms. Thompson.

"Thank you. Miss Newbury, I've come to you as a sort of absurd last resort because I know James Marshall very well and I know he couldn't have murdered Eve Harris." That was what it was, of course, realized Sally bleakly as she spoke, clutching her three Linton suspects and watching the expressionless white face. Brenda Newbury, curled up in an armchair with her arms folded tightly across her chest, looked even narrower than she had looked at the door. "I'm quite desperate for him, actually." The face still didn't change, but it was an enormous relief to have said it to someone who wasn't Gill or Peter. Sally leaned forward. "Miss Newbury, someone must have intercepted the correspondence between James and Eve Harris, and then impersonated James." Nothing even now, but she must still be careful. "Of course, this could have happened at James's end, it's more likely perhaps that it did, but you knew Eve and all about her marriage enterprise and I just felt I had to talk to you. You'll have told the police of course all they asked you about her but they think they've got their culprit and I imagine their questions must have been pretty routine. I'd like to ask you for everything you know about Eve, who her other friends were and who else might have known what she was doing. You said on TV you were her best friend. . . ."

At last there was a reaction. A cold little laugh that scarcely affected the mouth, let alone the eyes.

"Oh, yes. That."

"It isn't true?"

"Eve didn't appear to have any other friends, so you could say it was."

"You *did* say."

The eyes were dark and deepest, but Sally thought there was a flash of life from them. "I did, yes, I was shocked and sorry. I felt I could have been kinder to her when she was alive. The classic reaction of remorse." A ghost of a self-mocking smile. "It was absurd, though, we never even met outside work, and wouldn't have wanted to do the same things if we had."

"She confided in you?"

"She confided in everyone, she was utterly self-absorbed. I just happened to be around more consistently than other people. No!" The weary vigour made Sally jump. "There was more than that, Eve was fond of me, she was warmhearted." For an unnerving moment the face twisted as if in pain but recovered so quickly and completely that within seconds Sally was wondering if she had imagined it. "What makes you think James Marshall didn't kill her?" Even now Brenda Newbury wasn't really asking a question.

"Because I know him, and I know he isn't capable of killing."

"You're in love with him?" Not distaste, exactly, but an even stronger indication of detachment. Whatever Brenda Newbury gave Sally about Eve she would give her nothing for her own comfort. And had in fact just queried the foundation of Sally's faith in James's innocence.

"Yes. But that has nothing to do with it."

"So what was *he* doing, advertising for a wife with you around?"

"We're old friends, James and I, we knew one another when my husband and his wife were alive. That's how he still feels, but my feelings have changed. Another classic situation." Her rueful smile half drew one in return, strengthening her impression that Brenda Newbury's head would respond before her heart.

"But you still insist he didn't kill Eve?"

"I know he didn't. What I feel about him, what he doesn't feel about me, that has nothing to do with it. He isn't a killer."

"You may be wrong."

"No!" Sally saw her hands out towards Brenda, imploring. "James didn't kill Eve Harris. If you could just tell me . . . I saw a woman who lived on her landing. She said Eve's last boyfriend disappeared weeks ago. . . ."

"He did. I can give you his name and where he works, but after a few months in and out of bed with her he'd hardly deceive her with a beard, false or real. And he'd gone before she saw the ad."

"Is there anyone in your office who she hardly noticed but who noticed her? Someone who could have seen the correspondence and then stepped in?"

"It's hard to picture it, Mrs. Graham." Irony was back in the soft voice, but at least Brenda Newbury was going through the motions of considering the possibility. "Mr. Smith, our boss, is small and fat and totally without imagination. Sid the office boy came up to Eve's shoulder. One of the junior partners got married in February and never so much as noticed Eve's winning ways. She noticed his indifference, though, he could never have deceived her. And the other junior partner's a woman."

"That's all?"

"That's all."

Disappointment disappeared into the task of framing her next question. "Would you know if Eve left her correspondence with James in or on her desk at any time? You told me she confided in everyone, so I presume everyone would know what she was up to. Perhaps as a joke . . . Someone could have taken the bones out of it and handed them on to—to someone else. A joke that went wrong . . ." She tried to look casually into the dark eyes, but Brenda Newbury seemed hardly aware of her, let alone the inference of what she was saying. Hardly to be listening. "Miss Newbury?"

"As far as I can remember Eve always put the correspondence back in her bag and her bag always went with her when she was called for dictation." It was as if Brenda was according Sally just enough of herself to maintain social contact. "Someone would have had to have a very quick memory. If James Marshall didn't kill Eve, Mrs. Graham, I think the killer must still have come from Linton."

"Yes. I think he must." Sally made herself smile, bravely. "I'm sorry to have bothered you, Miss Newbury. I wouldn't have come if I hadn't been desperate. I've never felt so alone."

"You would, wouldn't you, on this one."

"Perhaps not if I had a brother or sister." She was pleased at the way she'd made use of Brenda's cool response and there was no chance for the moment of inducing tears, but head down she rummaged in her bag for a handkerchief and buried her face in it. "Do you have any brothers or sisters?" she asked through the folds.

"I have a brother."

Over the top of the handkerchief Sally saw the face stiffen, the eyes snap shut. Then open again to stare out of sight as they had been staring when Brenda Newbury had opened her front door.

"Are you close?" asked Sally. She blew her nose.

"We used to be." The eyes were on her again, as idly. "I don't see much of him now."

"That's a shame. He's married?"

"He's busy." Brenda was on her feet. "Are you feeling better? Can I get you some coffee? Brandy?"

"Thank you, I'm all right now. And I'm meeting a friend." There was nothing more to be learned from Brenda Newbury, and it was after half-past six. Sally got up too. "Thank you for being so patient."

"It wasn't difficult. I'm going to give you some brandy."

"Oh! Thank you." Blowing her nose again, Sally took a few steps towards the window as Brenda went over to a sideboard and a tray with bottles and glasses. The room no longer seemed so light, but there was no blue at all now in the sky, and across the narrow, car-choked street loomed another mansion block. On the table in the bay was a bowl of wizened fruit. And, symmetrically at an angle to it, two shiny parallel lines, one long and one short, breaking the film of dust.

"Here you are."

"Thanks."

Brenda had poured for herself as well and they drank quickly and in silence.

"You were right, that *has* helped." Sally set her glass down. "Goodbye, and thank you again."

"Goodbye."

The front door had closed before Sally started down the stairs. She was still on them when she realized to her surprise that she might have liked Brenda Newbury.

The complete Brenda whom she hadn't met. Who hadn't got something on her mind so disturbing that nothing else was real, even an oblique accusation of complicity to murder.

She couldn't quite make herself believe Brenda's preoccupation had anything to do with Eve Harris's death, but she had a specific request for Peter Matthews.

CHAPTER EIGHTEEN

The rain came, in large, sparse drops, when she was halfway back along the High Street. In her new world it was a phenomenon, and Sally stood still in surprise.

Alongside a newsagent's pitch. The piles of evening papers brought her sickeningly to attention, and then she read the shaky black letters on the hoarding.

I COULD HAVE BEEN THE FIRST VICTIM SAYS WOULD-BE BRIDE.

She didn't want to read any more, but she was fumbling in her purse. Standing there as the raindrops came more quickly, holding a copy of the *Evening Standard* and seeing that the headline was as big as the text underneath it. Moving into the shelter of a shop porch only because the rain, suddenly torrential, was threatening to obliterate the front page.

There was one small paragraph, reporting an armed robbery, which wasn't about James. The rest of the page explained that before he had met Eve Harris another woman had answered his *Times* advertisement and had been lucky to escape with her life.

I ran screaming along the pavement somewhere in Hampstead. I've never been so thankful to see a taxi.

From chagrin rather than fear. But the taxi driver might fancy being in on the act, and during the evening someone on radio or TV was bound to have screamed. . . .

The moment she was inside the hotel Peter sprang into sight, and Sally burst into tears. He sent her to the ladies' room and went to the bar to order her a double dry martini.

By the time she joined him she had almost recovered, and the *Evening Standard* was buried in a bin among the paper towels she had used to dry her hair.

"You saw the *Standard.*" His smile was still professional, but he patted her shoulder as they sat down. "I'm so sorry. Did you see Cyril, and Eve Harris's neighbours and Brenda Newbury?"

"Yes." She took a long swallow, trying to relax.

"Breathe deeply and tell me about them."

"I need to. Peter, Cyril may be James's nephew, but he's appalling. Frightened of his own shadow and for his own skin. I didn't quite accuse him, but when I suggested he might have taken the correspondence for a joke and shown it to someone I thought he was going to have a stroke. So I left it at that. But he's prepared to believe James killed Eve simply because the police believe it, James himself doesn't come into it. He was much worse than Harry, although of course he didn't frighten me the way Harry did. At least Harry talked about loving James as much as he'd always done —he used the word *love*—and said that if James denied the charge he'd believe him. Cyril's accepted the official case, and all his energies now are concentrated on trying to limit the damage to himself. Harry showed a sort of loyalty which when I thought about it afterwards I couldn't help being impressed by. I can't accept that James might be guilty. Harry can, and feels no different. I—"

"Sally, if Cyril or Harry killed Eve Harris, their reaction to James's arrest was an act."

She shook her head, bewildered. "I know, and then I forget. One of them's being so terribly clever. And that would be Harry, wouldn't it? Unless Cyril's fear on his own account has lifted him above himself. And there's Michael. I rang Mrs. Moxon when I left Cyril, and he was being odder than usual; she was worried."

"Oh?"

"Staring into space, not answering the telephone. That could be because of me, yesterday. Whether he's guilty or innocent. But Peter, Michael's the only one I can actually imagine being suddenly violent. I know I shouldn't say that, but—"

"But that's how you feel. And in that case you've got to consider it. And from what you've told me, Michael *isn't* like other people. Any joy at the café?"

"Yes!" She heard the determination in her voice. "The proprietor actually admitted that if he'd seen the photograph I showed him of James in another context he wouldn't have recognized it. When the police showed it to him he said it was the man who had been

there with Eve because there was nothing about it to say it wasn't.
If you see what I mean."

"I do, and it might just help. What about The Laurels?"

"The woman who lives across the landing from Eve—a Ms.
Thompson—let me in when I said I wasn't a reporter. She was in a
dressing gown and gave the impression of hardly ever getting out
of bed. The TV was in the sitting room and she didn't recognize
me. And she didn't hold any brief for Eve, they fell out months ago
because of Eve having pinched one of her boyfriends. I can't think
she'd have told me that if she knew anything about Eve's death.
She told me the rest of the place was elderly spinsters and widows.
It all seemed all right but I suppose that doesn't mean it was. Will
you—"

"I'll get in there. Brenda Newbury?"

Gin on brandy was beginning to distance her from the obscenity
of the *Evening Standard*'s front page. "Peter, it was extraordinary,
it was as if she wasn't there. I appeared out of the blue and she—
well, she didn't even seem surprised, let alone angry or upset. Even
when I was implying she could have taken the correspondence
herself. Well, made a note of it. She made me think of an actress
who'd learned her lines well enough to say them, but not to put
any expression in. Can you imagine what I mean?"

"I think so. So she gave you nothing?"

"Nothing. At least . . . Oh, nothing."

"Come on!"

"Well . . . I'm certain something was worrying her, but I can't
really believe it had anything to do with Eve or James or me, she
was already miles away when she opened her front door."

"You didn't get any clue as to what it might be?"

"No. Except . . . I just thought I'd find out if she had a
brother. She'd hardly have shown the Eve–James correspondence
to a boyfriend, so it seemed to me a brother might have been a
motive. Oh, I know it sounds absurd. . . ."

"No. Go on."

"Thanks. I made an opportunity to ask her—lamenting about
being an only child—and she . . . well, she just said yes, but it
wasn't what she said, it was the way she looked. She shut her eyes,
and when she opened them she was staring miles through me the

way she'd been when she let me in. For a while she'd at least looked at me, although she hardly seemed to be listening to what I said and I was surprised, somehow, the few times she answered a question. Anyway, when she told me she had a brother I just got the feeling that whatever it was that was bothering her had to do with him."

"Could be interesting."

"There was another thing." Sally paused to drink deeply. She was beginning to feel light-headed and welcomed the sensation. "I'm sure I'm being ridiculous but—"

"I'll be the judge of that."

"Thanks again. It's just . . . Her place hadn't been dusted for a while. I didn't feel it was chronically dirty like Ms. Thompson's, just a bit neglected. It seemed to go with her distraction, as if there was something so awful she'd forgotten about the everyday. Oh, I'm just being silly—"

"Carry on." His smile encouraged her.

"There was a table by the window covered in dust. Thick enough to show where something had been taken off." And clearer to her still than the people sitting round them. "Two parallel lines symmetrical to a bowl of fruit which I thought showed it was something that was normally there all the time. Peter, it must have been a photograph. The longer line the photograph itself, the shorter one the back support, there was just the right distance between them. The lines were so obvious and shiny the photograph could only just have been removed. A photograph of her brother? Whipped away when she heard her front doorbell?" He wasn't laughing, but she dropped her eyes. "I know I sound crazy, she was probably upset about her brother for some reason that had nothing to do with Eve Harris. She might even have thought I was him and put the photograph away so that he'd know she was angry with him."

"Y-e-e-s," he said judicially.

"But I won't rest until I know what he's like, whether he fits the man with the beard. If he does you can investigate him, and if he doesn't we can forget about him."

"Look, Sally." He put his hand on her arm. "You'll hate me for this and it doesn't mean I've lost faith in you, that I won't go on helping you, it's just something I feel I have to say."

"What is it?" She knew what it was, and shrugged her arm free.

Another bracing smile. "In view of the report tonight in the *Standard,* couldn't it just be that there's no need to look for anyone else, in London or Linton? That James found himself in a situation most of us never reach? Two neurotic women not really knowing what they wanted, encouraging him then suddenly repulsing, taunting him . . ."

"No!"

"Eve Harris could even have attacked him and forced him to act in self-defence."

"He'd have said so! He'd have told the police! Even Harry—if he's innocent—doesn't believe James could lie! And this woman now in the *Standard.* Peter, don't you *see?* If what she says was true it would take James even further out of character than the murder. It wouldn't be one terrible aberration, it would be the action of a man who hated women! And that man could never, never be James. Oh, Peter, don't you *see?"*

"I suppose I do." He drained his drink. "I knew I was on to a loser really, Sally, but I wanted to be absolutely sure you weren't wavering. Now, I've something for you."

"What?" Her heartbeat was suddenly too heavy for her chest.

"I also found out today that Brenda Newbury has a brother. His first name's Malcolm and he lives on his own in one of the blocks of flats which were built at the docks long before they became fashionable. He's an entrepreneur on the way to the big time, and he has a beard. Here, steady on! Waiter!"

"I'm all right."

"But we'll both have another drink."

"Thanks. Is he . . . Is he tall?"

"That I didn't discover. Or just how much hair he has. Apart from the beard!" He was looking anxiously into what must be her fanatically eager face. "Sally, if you don't keep in mind how remote this all is from Eve Harris's death you could be desperately disappointed."

"I know, I know. But I have to see him before I can dismiss him."

"You can't call on him the way you called on Brenda. You'll have to leave it to me to—"

"I want to see him for myself." She was pulling at his sleeve. "Peter, you're a journalist, you must have got to see people under false pretences before now."

"Yes, but haven't you done enough for today?"

"I will have when I've seen Malcolm Newbury. Have you got something on this evening?"

"No. All right, Sally. I'll begin by phoning him." The waiter put their drinks down and exchanged the bowl now empty of the olives Sally had been gulping for a fresh, full one. Sally lost the fight to pay. "You stay here and try to relax, build up your nerves, you may need them."

When he got back, the second bowl of olives and Sally's glass were almost empty.

"Well?"

"Answerphone. With the news that he'll be available after the weekend. Needless to say I didn't leave a message. We'll sleuth him to a pub or somewhere when he's around. All right?"

"I'd rather break into his flat tonight."

"You're obsessed, aren't you?" But she thought she saw admiration in his eyes. "And he might not actually be away."

"In which case we'll see what size and shape he is when he answers the door to hear us say wrong flat. If there's no answer we can at least find out whether or not his place is impregnable. And if it is you can always charm a spare key out of a neighbour."

"In one of those setups? And we won't find out what size he is if he isn't there."

"We can look at his clothes. If they don't fit that'll be the end of him. If they do—we can look at his letters. Peter, please!"

"All right, all right, we'll go to his flat."

"And if he's not there . . ."

"If a felony's possible, I'll commit it. As an investigative journalist I've developed something of a talent for illegal entry over the years. But don't let yourself get too excited, the London docks are still a tough area and Malcolm Newbury'll have been a fool not to lock his place up properly." He took her arm again, encouraged her to her feet. "You're fit enough to keep cool?"

"Yes. *Yes!*"

"Come along, then. Aren't you glad you shook off the other journalists?"

Out on the shiny grey street the rain had steadied to a drizzle. The usual wet-weather dearth of taxis affected them for no more than ten minutes, during which Sally discovered she had stopped drinking at just the right moment, with courage and confidence heightened and reactions apparently unimpaired.

"Flat sixty-five," said Peter in the taxi. "That sounds like at least the sixth floor. If there's a lift that's working I suggest we take it as far as the fifth and if I'm right you get out there and come warily up the stairs, then lurk at the top. I'll carry on in the lift, see what I can do, and come and tell you whether it's success or failure. Expect failure, in which case we'll descend the stairs together and hope the lift's still waiting at the floor below."

"And if it's success you'll whirl me inside."

"Sally, this is crazy! You've got Harry and Michael and Cyril."

"Malcolm Newbury's blotting them out."

"Only because you don't want a murderer in your seaside paradise."

She turned to him in surprise. "Is that what it is?"

"I think so. I can understand."

"And as Mrs. Moxon said, anything can happen in London." She was surprised, too, to hear herself laugh, but all at once she was feeling almost light-hearted.

Maxwell Gardens was a gaunt, upended rectangle in stained concrete set in a narrow band of unfeatured grass. The entrance door was missing a pane of glass and swung open at Peter's touch. There was no one to be seen outside the building, and no one in the small graffiti-decorated lobby. A square of cardboard on which a biro had written "Out of Order" hung askew on the scarred green door of one of the two lifts, but when Peter pressed the button beside the other it groaned open.

"On the way to the top, did you say?" whispered Sally as they got in.

"We'll look at the numbers on the fifth floor."

"I meant Malcolm Newbury. You said he was on the way to the top."

"That's what I heard. Perhaps he likes the anonymity."

"He's certainly got that."

The lift wavered and stopped. "Fifth floor." The door opened grudgingly onto a narrow corridor, and flat number fifty-eight. "As I thought. Out you get, Sally."

The stairs, beside the lift, were pitted black where the small squares of off-white mosaic were missing.

"Must have been a showplace once," said Peter, looking at them, "or it would have been unadorned concrete. And now that the docks are the place to be they'll be restoring it. On your way. Hover at the top. All right?"

"Never better." She knew it was the alcohol responding, but she was still in charge.

"See you soon."

She heard the lift jerk to life as she started up the stairs. Half-way there was a pause where they turned, and a dirty window she could see out of when she stood on tiptoe. Building skeletons and cranes and elegant warehouses already turned into homes beside the grey river, shrouded into mystery by the window dust and the low grey sky. She made herself stand there for two minutes by her watch, straining for sounds and hearing nothing above the faint deep hum which was the heart of the ugly giant that had swallowed them. When she reached the top of the flight she peered round at the corridor, surrealistically long and empty in both directions, forcing her shivering withdrawal. Peter found her leaning against the wall with her eyes shut.

"Sally! Success!"

"I just knew it!" She was instantly restored.

"No reply and nothing but a Yale lock! Malcolm Newbury doesn't deserve to be unburgled. I suppose he thought he was remote enough from the ground and the walkways. Walk *quickly!*"

The blue door marked sixty-five was just into a narrower corridor, and ajar. Peter urged her through it and closed it quietly behind them.

"It's better inside than out." The hall carpet was thick and fairly new, and she passed an elegant table and a bowl of spring flowers on her cautious way towards the light. "This must be the sitting room."

He followed her in. "Yes. Bit of a depressing view."

"Not as good as the other side, but I like the sheer size of it, I've always thought the size of the view would be a compensation for high-rise living." She turned her back on the window. "I sound like an estate agent. Let's go through the place, Peter, then start looking properly."

"Whatever you say." He took her hand, led her back into the hall where there were four other white doors, all of them closed. Sally left the opening of them to Peter, and the first entry. "Separate WC. Next door to well-appointed bathroom. Newbury keeps the place in pretty good order for a man on his own."

It was strange, she thought, that this should be her first time of wondering if Peter Matthews was on his own, too. But although he was her lifeline and they'd become friends after a fashion, they were really only thinking of each other as means to the end which had absorbed every moment of their time together.

The other doors concealed a small, tidy kitchen and one equally neat bedroom with sunbed predominant.

"Brenda's place would have been like this," said Sally on the last threshold, "if she hadn't been knocked sideways."

"It's quite decent, isn't it? Easier to believe once you shut the front door that Malcolm Newbury's on the up and up."

"Yes. Although most things would seem good after the approach. Where shall we start?"

"Let's start with a drink. I could do with one after joining the criminal classes."

"You implied you'd broken and entered before. And if we have a drink we'll be thieves as well as trespassers."

"Lambs into sheep. We've already crossed the line. Come on."

"Just a minute. We may not have to start at all."

She pulled her hand free and led the way back into the bedroom. "You're not quite as tall as James, Peter, and nothing like as broad, but you'll do as a rough model." She grinned at him, energy bounding in her at the opportunity of doing something, however obliquely, for James. She opened a white internal door onto a neat row of suits and jackets, pulled out a suit. "Let's try this." She threw the jacket onto the bed, held the trousers against him. "Well, they look the right length, so Malcolm seems to qualify on height. Try the jacket."

"I don't need to." He picked it up and looked inside. "Standard size. My size. It seems Mr. Newbury is still in the running."

"Yes." Hands suddenly trembling, she restored the suit clumsily to its hanger and pushed them into the cupboard. "I will have a drink, Peter."

Back in the sitting room she flopped onto the sofa and looked round her. "No photographs." Peter was crossing another good carpet towards a corner cupboard. "No personality, really. All one can tell about Malcolm Newbury is that he's very clean and tidy." The corner cupboard yielded a sight of glasses and bottles. "Right first time, Peter, well done."

"Gin and dry?"

"Please. I know I'm drinking as much today as I normally drink in a week, but the circumstances are unusual. And it's the first time I've done anything criminal."

"You're only an accessory to a crime. Which should carry a very light sentence." Smiling, he brought the glass across to her, wiping the bottom of it with a clean white handkerchief before setting it down on the small table beside the sofa.

"You may have opened Malcolm's door, but it's you who are the accessory, I'm the mastermind." She was talking too much, too stupidly, but it didn't matter. "Thank you, Peter. Oh, good luck!"

Back by the cupboard he picked up his whisky, nodded over the rim of the glass. "Cheers!"

She drank, then put her glass down. "It's no good, I can't sit still all the way through that, I want to get started. On that bureau, it's like a magnet." She got to her feet. "And the longer we stay the more we're tempting fate. I know Malcolm Newbury gave the impression on his answerphone that he was away for the weekend, but anything could happen to make him change his mind and come home early."

"He won't do that, Sally, I promise you." Another reassuring smile. "You see, he's here already."

CHAPTER NINETEEN

He didn't try to stop her running to the front door, but of course it was locked. He followed her out to the hall, tossing a bunch of keys about in his hand.

"I'm terribly sorry, Sally." Her back was against the door, and he put his free hand on the wall beside her. Not threateningly, the worst thing was that he was still as he had always been, his smile as cheering. "Come and sit down."

Like a zombie she obeyed him, aware somewhere beyond the numbness that Linton was innocent. Harry and Michael and Cyril, as well as James, had meant what they said, were ordinary people. Even awaiting death, as she must be, she was glad to know that.

He saw her back on to the sofa, put the keys carefully into a porcelain dish. "Three of them," he said, "for the moment. When the place is upgraded I shan't need three, of course, there'll be a man on the door."

"I ought to have waited for Gail Prestwick." She was astonished by her calm, quiet voice.

"You did, Sally." He sat down on the other side of the room, leaned confidingly towards her. "That was clever, wasn't it? By inventing Gail Prestwick I was actually able to walk away from you, have you call me back. And if you hadn't, she wouldn't have shown up and I'd still have been around the next morning."

"You—wrote that letter?"

"Of course. You weren't so impressive at your conference as I made you believe, Sally." Even in these last moments of her life she felt the jolt to her self-esteem. "You've made it so easy for me all along, you even begged me help you walk into my parlour." He was on his feet; she had flinched as he passed the sofa to reach the window and stand staring out. "I tried to give you a last chance tonight in the hotel, but I think really that as soon as you noticed me in Linton police station it was inevitable we'd end up here together. It would have been different if I'd stayed away, and I wish now that I had, you're a nice person, Sally." He turned to smile at her. "But I didn't. I couldn't. I had to see what happened when they found the body. And you had to find another murderer. And so when you came to London and saw Brenda Newbury's brother you'd have recognized the journalist you saw in Linton, and you'd have known. Another drink." He came and took her glass. His smile now seemed permanent, but with an edge of gravity. He crossed to the drinks cupboard and poured slowly and carefully. "Here you are." He set the glass back on the small table beside her, primitive anaesthetic to prepare her for the amputation of her life.

There was probably no one within earshot, and anyway she couldn't shout out, it would make him do whatever he was going to do more quickly, more brutally, than he appeared to be intending, back again relaxed in his chair by the bureau whose contents she no longer needed to see. How would he get rid of her body?

"Come on!" She had blacked out long enough for him to have got back to her, to be trying to get some of the new drink between her lips. She wished now he'd taken such a good opportunity, got it over while she wouldn't have known. "Brenda had the right idea, giving you brandy, we ought to have stuck to it."

"I'm all right." She struggled to sit upright, command her mind. "You rang Brenda when you said you were going to ring—yourself."

"Yes. That was a tricky bit, getting you to accept a businessman who'd inform the world via his answerphone that his flat would be burglar-friendly over the weekend. But you'd had a few drinks on a one-track mind." He was crossing the room again, mercifully away from her. "I rang Brenda because I wanted to be sure you'd been telling me the truth about what went on between you, and I wanted Brenda to know you'd forced me to bring you here. I was worried about her, too. You reassured me on the whole, but there were one or two things . . . She's very bright, but she hasn't managed herself too well over this."

"Brenda—knows?" He was back in his chair, and she was glad again there were a few moments left.

"She does now. When she went on television calling herself Eve

Harris's best friend I thought it was time I put her in the picture. Unfortunately the damage was done, she'd caught your attention."

"Why did you kill Eve Harris, Malcolm?"

"Because she asked for it." He looked surprised by her question. "I didn't want to kill her any more than I wanted to kill that other girl." If she had had any hope, with those words she lost it. "I've never wanted to kill a girl. But Eve Harris was a drab, she took me down on the shore and made up to me. Then when I—she turned on me, she was scratching me, tearing my tie. I tried to control her, calm her down. I had my hands on her neck, there's a spot there, everyone's heard of it, I must have pressed it."

She wouldn't remind him Eve Harris had been strangled. "Like with the other girl?"

"Yes! She turned on me, too. When Eve Harris died I planned to put the blame on James Marshall. And he'd started it, I was with Eve because of him."

She couldn't begin to attack his crazy logic. "Why did you impersonate James?"

"Because I'd seen Eve's photograph and because I had the chance, of course! Brenda photocopied the correspondence and Marshall's photograph to show me—"

"Brenda . . ."

"Brenda shows me everything, shares everything with me." He was impatient, she ought to have known. "She wasn't thinking I'd do anything with them. But Eve had given Brenda a copy of the photograph she'd had taken for Marshall, and Brenda put it on show. As a picture she said, because it was so decorative. You were right, Sally, there was a photograph on that table, but it was of Eve. I had to remind Brenda on the phone to put it away before you came, she wasn't noticing things—"

"Eve!" Sally heard the hard rasp of her laughter, and took another drink. At least she'd been offered anaesthetic of a kind, if she took enough she would pass out. Not yet, though, she'd prefer to die as knowledgeable as possible. And as far into the future.

"Yes. Eve. When I was at Brenda's I couldn't stop looking at it. Every time she went out to the kitchen I had to get up and go over to that photograph. And then when she showed me Marshall's stuff . . ."

His hand closed sharply round the arm of his chair, and Sally drank again. She was at last beginning to drift away, she had to concentrate to hold him in her gaze. "Yes, I can see, you were bound to do it, weren't you?"

"Of course I was. You're very understanding, Sally, far more understanding than Brenda. And she of all people ought to have understood, she'd handed Eve to me on a plate. It was so easy."

"Of course. How did you—plan—to keep the deception going?" Her voice, now, was a lazy slur.

"I wouldn't have needed to, once Eve was in love with me. It shouldn't have taken long. . . ." For an instant, memory clouded his confident face, but it cleared as he leaned towards Sally. "It's a shame, Sally, we could have been such good friends, it's only when I want to make love to a girl that things tend to go wrong. I get angry, you see. But I like you enormously and we get on so well together. You might even have got me going again with my painting. You'll understand, though, as things are . . ." Regret entered the smile.

She hiccuped. "Except you said if the murderer killed me as well he'd prove his case, bring the police down on him rather than just one silly—one bloody silly woman."

"Yes, but I was meaning—"

"I know, you were meaning other people. You're cleverer than other people, o' course."

"That's it." He smiled his approval. "I've made sure these past two days that you openly saw everyone who could have killed Eve Harris. Except for me, no one knows you went as far as seeing Malcolm Newbury, he won't be one of the new suspects."

She heard the yelp of laughter before she realized it was hers. "When I said . . . When I said I wannid to break into this flat I saw admir—admiration in your eyes. I thought it was for my single . . . Oh, God . . . My sin—gle-mind—ed—ness, but it was for your own cleverness, wa'n't it?"

"I expect so."

She tried to sit upright. "How you going to get my body out of here?" She didn't want to know, but the longer they talked the longer there wouldn't be one.

"I'm not sure yet, but Brenda will help me, she loves me so much she'd do anything for me."

Would she? Hazily remembering those blank eyes, Sally wondered. Then realized there was something else she wanted to die knowing. "Was it a real beard?"

"Oh, yes. I grew it after that first girl died. Then shaved it off after Eve. Brenda was delighted, she never liked it. You and Brenda would have got on well. . . . Oh, Sally, you're so bright and such fun, I'm sorry!"

"You could let me go." It was just something to say. And anyway, she didn't think she would be able to get up.

"You know I couldn't. You wouldn't let your precious James carry the can."

"Could I have another drink?" She watched him at the cupboard. "There's one thing per—perhaps you haven't thought of."

"What's that?" He turned sharply, catching the glass against the key in the cupboard door. The glass shattered, spraying its fresh contents in all directions. "Hell and damnation!"

It was the first time she had seen him out of control. She sat relaxed, locked to the sofa, half watching him, the way since Tom died she had half watched late-night films on television, as he ran in and out of the room with kitchen paper, soap, a bowl of water, crawling after the slivers of glass which gleamed like diamonds among the thick pile of his pale carpet, tenderly ministering to it. She wondered if he would notice if she picked up the bunch of keys, walked to the front door, opened it and ran away, but she didn't know how the keys worked, and anyway her body wouldn't make it. She thought ten minutes had gone by on the blurred face of his wall clock when he filled another glass and placed it on the table beside her.

"What were you going to say to me, Sally?" It was as if the interruption had been as vital and unremarkable as breathing.

"I was going to say . . ." Now that she was almost ready to pass out she was fighting it, trying to concentrate. "You been seen with me a' the Granhotel having dinner, by a lorra people. When I disappear they'll remember you, and they'll find you even if you grow another beard."

"They won't, you know, Sally." His smile was infinitely compassionate. "Peter Matthews doesn't exist, and where would they look? And you'll be found in Linton. After several days out at sea. By which time anyway it might look like an accident."

It was worse after Mal had telephoned, put it into words. *Don't worry, Bebe, I'll take care of her.* He'd given her something to keep saying, over and over and over, as she paced the room. *Don't worry, Bebe, I'll take care of her. Take care of her, take care of her, take care of her.*

It had all been a mistake, of course, just as it had been that earlier time. Mal hadn't meant to kill Eve Harris any more than he'd meant to kill that other girl. Sally Graham would be all right, he wouldn't—he couldn't—do anything in cold blood, it was only when he got carried away . . . He was clever, he'd be able to neutralize her without doing anything drastic, get her back to Linton to carry on her amateur detective work until she ran out of steam.

Don't worry, Bebe, I'll take care of her. . . . She'd said the words so often they were beginning to lose meaning.

Mal had been crazy, inventing Peter, he should have laid low, and then if Sally Graham had found her way to his door of her own accord he'd have been no more than the brother of the murdered woman's office mate.

Murder! Mal! Bent double, Brenda staggered to a chair, clutching at the fresh shaft of pain as she relived the agony of learning what Mal had done. To Eve. To that girl three years ago. He'd arrived with champagne, she'd thought there was something to celebrate, and when he'd given her enough to make her feel almost light-hearted, he'd told her. And reassured her.

Don't worry, Bebe, I'll take care of her.

No!

Brenda tottered to the window and pushed it wider, lurched back to her chair. If he'd told her right away what had happened she'd have warned him to stay away from Linton, not push luck as good as he'd had the first time. . . . If only she hadn't duplicated James Marshall's photograph and those letters he'd sent Eve, then shown them to Mal as she showed him everything, told him every-thing. But she hadn't so much as dreamed what he would do.

She ought to have done. She hadn't seen much of Mal since he'd gone off on his own, but she knew him well enough. *It was just a bit of fun, Bebe. It was asking for it and I couldn't resist. Not after seeing that photograph! I was going to confess to her in the end, once she was hopelessly in love with me.*

In love . . . She was on her feet again, but only to fling herself down on the floor, spread herself out on her stomach on the carpet and writhe the agony of her jealousy and erotic longing. *Oh Mal, oh my darling, I'm in love with you, I can't hide from it any longer. That's why it was no good with Barry when it came to it, no good with anyone else.*

That was why it had hurt so when he told her about his women, why she had felt the unique sharp pain nothing else ever gave her. Why she was only half alive those long weeks and months when she didn't see him

Mal! She could ride the jealousy even now that it had a name. And so long as he was there she could be content to be his sister, sisters had it, really, over girlfriends and even wives, sisters were forever. He'd done terrible things, so terrible she was unable to think of them, but he was still Mal, still her beloved.

Don't worry, Bebe, I'll take care of her. . . .

If he didn't, if he let Sally Graham go to the police, Mal would be lost to her and to himself for the rest of their lives. They'd send him to a special sort of prison, to a living death. Mal, her darling!

And if he did . . .

Don't worry, Bebe.

Brenda pressed her hands against her ears.

"Wanna drink."

Sally stretched her hand in the direction of her glass. Quickly, before she could knock it over, he had hold of it and was offering it to her lips.

"Sorl right. Don't fuss." She drained it, spilling a little on her chin. She really was on the way out now, the drink had got there first. Which was probably what he'd intended should happen, she believed him that he didn't want to kill her.

But he'd taken the glass away, taken it across the room and put it down by the cupboard, she'd had all the anaesthetic she was going to get. An alarm bell rang very faint and far away. "Look," she said, as he came back. "Don't . . . don't . . . You don' have to . . ."

He had pulled her to her feet, he was supporting her. By the neck. She was too heavy, though, she was falling back onto the sofa. He wasn't trying to lift her again, he was letting her lie back and was leaning over her, resting his hands on her shoulders.

"I'm so sorry, Sally."

"Look. You don' have to . . ."

"I'm afraid I do."

She thought his hands had moved to her neck, but she was too sleepy to be certain. His face was so close to hers it was blurred, she couldn't see it, she only knew it was so large it was blotting out the light.

She tried to speak again but she could only gurgle, and all at once she was wanting to cough. All at once, too, she was recharged with energy and was using it to struggle, she had hands and legs which were moving, fighting. . . . But only as they did in dreams, as if under water.

The bell was still ringing, somewhere a long way off—the place where she was going?—and there was the sound of knocking. Was that how death came?

He heard himself curse, he didn't seem able to find the spot and there was shouting now as well as knocking and ringing. Voices calling "Police! Open up!" If he didn't go they'd break the door down.

Malcolm Newbury stepped back from the sofa, picked up his keys, and made his way briskly to his front door. It wasn't much of a door—when the place was upgraded he'd have a new one—but he'd prefer to keep it in one piece until then. He unlocked and opened it.

On the step were two policemen in uniform and an older man in a mackintosh.

"Malcolm Newbury?"

"Yes. Of course. What can I do for you, gentlemen?"

They gave him their names, showed him a card. "Is a Mrs. Sally Graham in your flat, Mr. Newbury?"

"Certainly she is, Chief Inspector."

"We'd like a word with her, Mr. Newbury. May we come in?"

They started to crowd past him before he had a chance to answer them. "Really, Chief Inspector!" Shrugging, he shut the front door. "Straight ahead."

"Look at this, sir!"

The uniformed men were kneeling at the sofa, holding Sally between them. Her face was a bit of a funny colour, the only time he'd seen it flushed, but then she'd been drinking his gin all evening.

"I'm afraid she's a bit the worse for wear, Chief Inspector."

"She's half strangled, Mr. Newbury."

One of the policemen had dashed out of the room, was back with a glass of water before the other had managed to undo Sally's blouse. She choked over the water and the chief inspector said, "Thank God!"

"She'll be all right, sir."

"I told you," said Malcolm. "She must have had half a dozen gins with dry martini."

"Before you attempted to strangle her." The chief inspector, now, was sitting on the sofa holding Sally's hand, and the two uniformed men were standing very close to Malcolm, one on either side.

"If you'd come earlier," he said, "she'd have been absolutely all right. She's all right now."

"I'm sorry, sir."

The uniformed men took hold of his arms, and he felt his smile die. "I'll ring Brenda. Brenda'll explain it all."

"Your sister's already explained it," said the chief inspector from the sofa. "It was she who sent for us, told us to come quickly. She's on her way now to the station where we're taking you, you'll see her there."

"Brenda didn't send for you. Not Brenda."

"I'm afraid so, Mr. Newbury."

"Not Brenda!"

Malcolm Newbury buried his face in his hands and began to cry.

His heavy sobs were the first thing Sally heard as she reached the surface, his blind, blundering figure the first thing she saw as the uniformed men guided him to the door.

When the chief inspector had rung for a doctor he went out to the kitchen and came back with a cup of black coffee. "Take it slowly," he said. "You're all right."

"If he hadn't been so tidy, you'd have been too late." It hurt her throat horribly to talk, but she couldn't help it.

"I'm sorry, Mrs. Graham. I don't quite follow you."

"Tha's not surprising." The giggle swelled to the surface, trickled painfully out. "You see, I'm drunk." She gripped his hand as tears blurred his lovely, unsmiling face. "Not dead drunk, though."

CHAPTER TWENTY

The first TV interview was part of an early evening chat show, and took place before the marks of Malcolm's fingers had disappeared from Sally's neck.

The press, alerted by the chat show host, made much next morning of this visible evidence of her constancy, and the romance of a friendship transformed into love under the stress of a wrongful arrest proved powerful enough to carry the day with quality and tabloid alike.

"You're in the clear, children," said Harry at the first sustained meeting between the three of them. At Sally's suggestion it took place on neutral ground, at a London restaurant following recording of the second TV interview for an in-depth study of loyalty. She had feared it more than the interview. "Even the most cynical editor is unlikely now to query your story of how and when you met. Old friends for ever!" To her amazed relief he winked at her as he raised his glass.

"I'm starting to believe it myself." Her return offering was an uninhibited smile. "Although I'm glad we don't have to pretend with you, Harry. Or Mrs. Moxon."

"Mrs. Moxon! What's the latest there?" Harry looked from one to the other of them, which was as promising as the wink. She had to accept Harry, he was James's best friend, and if there could be a truce between them so much the better. There was no doubt he had lost out since her appearance on James's scene: his question about Mrs. Moxon was witness to the fact that he no longer crossed the White House lawn without an invitation. But by not telling James of the pass he had made at her Sally had evened the score. Harry had as much cause as she had to feel better as the lunch progressed.

"Poor Mrs. Moxon," said James. "Michael's broken his silence at last, but only to turn her out of her house. When I bought it for her she insisted it should be put in his name, worrying about him being all right if anything happened to her. Unfortunately she told him. She also told him about my enterprise and showed him my ad and the letter I'd written, she confessed when we'd taken her in after she arrived a couple of nights ago on the doorstep. She was getting so anxious he would never find a wife and that she'd leave him alone when she died, she just couldn't resist the opportunity. She told us she didn't set out to show him any of the photographs, but the fatal one of Eve was on the top and she saw his reaction to it. He's so often alone in the garden, with the back door unlocked and expected to come in for his tea, she was afraid he'd been tempted to have another look at it."

"It *was* hot stuff," said Harry. "Young Cyril was not a pretty sight taking it in."

"Cyril had no difficulty believing James had killed Eve," said Sally, partly to show Harry she was making a distinction between him and James's nephew by telling on Cyril. "The establishment believed it, which was enough for him. I've thought a lot about what you said, Harry, when you came that evening to the White House." They looked at one another, and she realized with a slight shock that any grit between them in the future would be her attraction for him rather than mutual animosity. She would just have to earn his respect as well, which might eventually neutralize it. She turned to James. "Harry was able to face the fact that you might have killed Eve, darling. As I wasn't. He told me that whether you had or not you were the same man, his friend. Then he said that if you told him you hadn't, he'd believe you. Part of me of course wanted to believe he'd killed her, but I remember that even then another part wanted that splendid sort of loyalty to be true."

"You were telling us about Mrs. Moxon," Harry reminded James. The colour in his face, the first Sally had seen there, could just be pleasure as well as embarrassment.

"Yes. Well, Michael had turned her out, she had a little old suitcase in her hand and asked if she could stay at the White House for the night. Of course we said she could stay until Michael relented, or she found somewhere else. Michael hasn't relented. I think he really doesn't want to have anything more to do with his mother, he can't forgive her for being able to imagine him as a murderer." He hoped he would eventually be able to forgive Harry the same offence. "She's devastated, of course. Trying to work it off by being even more thorough about the house, if that's possible. We've been glad she's had Heidi and Blackie to reconcile."

"How are they doing?"

"Very well." James tried to apologize to Harry with his eyes for having caused him to ask a second question to which before the advent of Sally he would have known the answer. "Which is more of a surprise to Mrs. Moxon than it is to Sally and me, she being used to her own feline demon. As far as the garden's concerned we've lost out, it's too close to her now for Michael. An ordinary chap just couldn't keep anger like that going, but Michael isn't ordinary and I suspect he will. I've a feeling, though, that in the long run they'll both be better off, they were choking one another. I'm negotiating with the council for a flat for Mrs. M. not far away, and meanwhile she's in the little bedroom."

"A very timely chaperon!" Harry spoke with mock severity, but real curiosity flashed across his eyes.

"We're getting married on Wednesday," said James quietly. The others didn't laugh when he looked furtively round him. "Eleven o'clock at Linton Register Office. We fixed it up yesterday. You'll look after me I hope, Harry, and Sally'll have Gill. Mrs. Moxon, having prepared a lunch at home, will be our wedding guest. Not another soul and not even a buttonhole, the press are still lurking."

"Not even Hilda and Cyril?" Harry's reaction was a complex mingling of envy, anger, regret and interested anticipation, all of which he kept easily out of his face.

"No. Too risky and they haven't earned it. We'll go and confess on Wednesday evening if we feel strong enough. Probably to the press as well, they haven't treated us badly."

"Have you decided what to do about the newspaper offer?"

"Yes. Nothing. It would be too much of a risk despite our expertise and anyway we'd rather not."

"You feel that too, Sally?"

"Goodness, yes!"

"Hm. Well, I expect you're wise, although the money . . . You're suing that woman, of course, for defamation?"

"A public recantation is imminent, Harry. It'll suffice."

"How unworldly you are, James. Yes, of course I'll be your best man. I hope you'll both be very happy." Sally hoped the mockery in Harry's eyes was too deep for James to notice, he wouldn't be looking for it. "It will be agreeable to meet that attractive daughter of yours again, Sally."

"She is lovely, isn't she?" Sally wished she could announce that Gill was bespoke, but Gill looked like being a free spirit a long way into the future. She must resist the temptation to tell her to look out for Harry It wasn't her business any more, and Gill could take care of herself.

"Are you going straight home?" Harry drained his second cup of coffee. "I thought I'd look in on that exhibition of domestic architecture at the Barbican."

"You're not going back to the office?"

"Heavens no, James, my diary's blank for the rest of the afternoon. We three round a table is a celebration, I wasn't going to spoil it with sordid glancings at my watch." Harry smiled genially from one to the other, confirming Sally's further suspicion that whenever he felt like unsettling her his means would be irony. "Like to join me, or have you had enough for today?"

"James is free," said Sally. "I've got an appointment."

"Sally wants to call and see Brenda Newbury."

"Brenda Newbury! She's agreed to see you?"

"I haven't been able to get hold of her, the appointment's with myself to call at her flat. Every time I ring her an answerphone suggests I leave a message and she'll ring me back. She doesn't. The police told me where she was working when—when she was with Eve, but when I rang them they said she was only a temp and had moved on. They gave me the name of the agency she works for, but all *they* could tell me was that she was taking a break. I've written. No reply."

"She's probably gone away," said Harry. "Best thing she could do. That brother of hers will never see the light of day again, she'll have to get used to it."

"Oh, she will, she's strong. But it must have been a fearful blow." Yet again she saw those blank eyes. "And when the trial comes up . . . She saved my life. I should have gone before now, happiness makes you selfish."

"That's true, Harry." Although no sensation was as strong in James as it had been before his arrest. Except tiredness. "I'll go with Sally if you don't mind. Not to go in with her unless she wants me to. Just for going home."

"Honestly, James . . ."

"Honestly I'd rather come." He was aware of relief and satisfaction that the lunch had gone so well. Sally hadn't said much, but he'd seen the cynicism in Harry's eyes the time he'd come to the prison, and he knew what he must have put her through. In a day or two he'd surely start experiencing the more important emotions as well. Like being glad he was home, and feeling he loved Sally as well as just knowing it. And taking in with more than his brain the fact that she had almost died for him.

"Thanks. You don't mind, Harry?"

"Of course I don't mind. I'll see you soon."

"Supper on Sunday?" Sally glanced at James, who smiled and nodded. "We'll be able by then to give you the precise wedding timetable." Which already included Gill coming up on Tuesday and mother and daughter spending the night in a double room at the Grand. Not just because it would look and feel right, it would also create the most favourable conditions for trying to dispel the last of Gill's doubts and assuring her she was as beloved as ever.

"I'll look forward to it. That was a splendid lunch, both of you."

On the short tube journey to Kensington evidence of recognition from a man sitting opposite started James trembling.

"Are you all right, darling?" She felt constrained to murmur. It would be a long time before they could lead a normal life. "Are you absolutely sure Wednesday isn't too soon for you?" He had asked her to marry him as soon as possible, but he was still convalescent.

"It's the one thing I am sure of. I'm only tired, Sally. And a bit bewildered. By coming out of the nightmare as well as going into it. It makes life feel a bit arbitrary, not quite real." He thought he might be better now he'd found the words to describe it. "You're sure this visit isn't going to upset you, darling?" Their anxious eyes met and to his relief they both laughed. "We're as bad as each other." Successive tube stops were adjusting the balance of their traumas, tipping it towards hers.

"Thank goodness! Yes, it probably is going to upset me but I have to see her. I should have made the effort days ago."

"You've done all you could to get hold of her."

"In a way."

"No one can make headway against an answerphone. And the police couldn't come up with any relatives."

"At least by going to her flat I may come up with a neighbour who'll be able to tell us if she's away or out or just not disconnecting that answerphone. If I draw a total blank I'll ring the prison, find out if and when she's visiting."

"And waylay her?"

"Well, yes. Just to say thank you. That's all I want."

This time in Kensington High Street it was dry. Sun was dazzling the shop windows, discovering tiny diamonds in the grey paving stones.

"She wasn't finding life quite real, either," said Sally, trying not to walk too fast. "I hope she still isn't."

"She has things to hide from," said James. "I haven't."

"No, darling. So you'll be better soon."

The side road was as busy as it had been the first time. Sally looked up at what she now knew to be Brenda Newbury's front window. "No net curtains, but you still can't see anything."

"You were hoping for a face at the window, weren't you? Sally, she must be away."

"Leaving the answerphone on would be a very good way to ignore the telephone if you were at home and couldn't face it live."

There were no milk bottles on the old coconut mat but a freebee newspaper was jammed in the letterbox.

They rang the bell several times, heard its sharp summons and listened to the restored silence.

Eventually James seized the newspaper and wrestled it out of sight. They heard the thud inside, heavier than the paper's weight. "Post was stuck in there too, she didn't reroute it. Perhaps I can see the extent of the pile-up."

The slit was at waist height and he had to crouch down to it. He stayed there so long Sally crouched too, trying to edge him aside. Then he straightened up, pulling her with him.

"What did you see? You saw something, James!" She was looking at his face.

"No, Sally! Please don't!" He had his back to the door.

"I must, I have to. James!"

"Yes, of course."

He stood aside, then, and she crouched again.

At first she couldn't think what they were, the brown tubes dangling side by side above the busily patterned carpet, bent identically at the ends and illumined by the light from the open sitting-room door. It was only when she noticed the shoes which had first seemed a part of the pattern that she realized they had fallen off Brenda's elegant narrow feet, hanging and very slightly swinging in the shaft of sunshine.

Eileen Dewhurst was born in Liverpool and educated at Huyton College, later Oxford. As a freelance journalist, she has published numerous articles in such periodicals as *The Times* and *Punch,* and her plays have been performed in England. *Dear Mr. Right* is her eleventh novel for the Crime Club.